"There's something between us, whether we like it or not,"

Alex said impatiently.

"And I gather you don't like it?" Gail snapped.

"Well, do *you?* I don't like anything about this whole situation, but for some reason or other you've gotten under my skin. I want you. I want you in my life, my arms and my bed. I won't let you make a fool of me, but anything else is yours for the asking."

Gail stared at him, unable to believe she'd heard right. "And just what, exactly, do you count as making a fool of you?"

"I'm a skilled campaigner. I offer the best—an apartment, jewels, a gold credit card—whatever your heart desires. Everything but marriage."

Dear Reader,

Spring is the perfect time to celebrate the joy of new romance. So get set to fall in love as Silhouette Romance brings you six new wonderful books.

Blaine O'Connor is a *Father in the Making* in Marie Ferrarella's heartwarming FABULOUS FATHERS title. When this handsome bachelor suddenly becomes a full-time dad, he's more than happy to take a few lessons in child rearing from pretty Bridgette Rafanelli. Now he hopes to teach Bridgette a thing or two about love!

Love—Western style—begins this month with a delightful new series, WRANGLERS AND LACE. Each book features irresistible cowboys and the women who tame their wild hearts. The fun begins with *Daddy Was a Cowboy* by Jodi O'Donnell.

In Carolyn Zane's humorous duet, SISTER SWITCH, twin sisters change places and find romance. This time around, sister number two, Emily Brant, meets her match when she pretends sexy Tyler Newroth is her husband in *Weekend Wife*.

Also this month, look for *This Man and This Woman*, an emotional story by Lucy Gordon about a wedding planner who thinks marriage is strictly business—until she meets a dashing Prince Charming of her own. And don't miss *Finally a Family*, Moyra Tarling's tale of a man determined to win back his former love—and be a father to the child he never knew he had. And Margaret Martin makes her debut with *Husband in Waiting*.

Happy Reading!

Anne Canadeo
Senior Editor

Please address questions and book requests to:
Silhouette Reader Service
U.S.: 3010 Walden Ave., P.O. Box 1325, Buffalo, NY 14269
Canadian: P.O. Box 609, Fort Erie, Ont. L2A 5X3

THIS MAN AND THIS WOMAN

Lucy Gordon

Silhouette
R O M A N C E™
Published by Silhouette Books
America's Publisher of Contemporary Romance

SILHOUETTE BOOKS

ISBN 0-373-19079-4

THIS MAN AND THIS WOMAN

Copyright © 1995 by Lucy Gordon

Printed in U.S.A.

LUCY GORDON

met her husband-to-be in Venice, fell in love the first evening and got engaged two days later. After twenty-three years they're still happily married and now live in England with their three dogs. For twelve years Lucy was a writer for an English women's magazine. She interviewed many of the world's most interesting men, including Warren Beatty, Richard Chamberlain, Sir Roger Moore, Sir Alec Guinness and Sir John Gielgud.

In 1985 she won the *Romantic Times* Reviewer's Choice Award for Outstanding Series Romance Author. She also won a Golden Leaf Award from the New Jersey Chapter of the RWA, was a finalist in the RWA Golden Medallion contest in 1988 and won the 1990 Rita Award in the Best Traditional Romance category for *Song of the Lorelei*.

Sir James and Lady Medway

request the honor of your presence

at the marriage of Miss Gail Rivers

to their son, Alexander Medway,

at St. Anthony's Church

Reception to follow at the Medway Estate

Kindly respond

Chapter One

"If you don't leave for the church now you'll be late," Gail said worriedly.

Freddie Medway, handsome in his wedding togs, checked his watch and sighed. "I warned Dad about the time ten minutes ago," he said. "But he's hanging on until the last moment. You can guess why."

"Your brother, Alex," Gail said with a grimace. "How can he be so unkind as to miss his own father's wedding?"

"You obviously don't know Alex or you couldn't ask that. Hardheaded, hard-hearted. Never mind feelings. Only the facts matter. And the facts, as far as Alex is concerned, are that Dad's been taken in by a scheming fortune hunter."

"And how would he know?" Gail demanded wrathfully. "Just because Liliane's a few years younger than Sir James—"

"Thirty years younger," Freddie said. "Which actually makes her younger than Alex and not much older than me."

"But she really seems to care for your father."

"That's what I told Alex. All right, maybe she wouldn't be marrying Dad if he was a poor man, and I expect she likes the idea of being Lady Medway. But if she's fond of him and makes him happy, surely that's all that counts?"

"But your brother thinks the worst of her?"

Freddie gave his impish grin. "Alex thinks the worst of everyone on principle. He says it saves time and inconvenience."

"He sounds a real charmer."

"Alex doesn't believe in charm," Freddie said at once. "It gets in the way of business. He tears his hair when I put myself out to be charming to customers. 'Just cut the cackle and make the sale,' he says. But sometimes the cackle helps the sale along."

Gail could believe it. At twenty-five Freddie Medway was good-looking, lighthearted and delightful. She'd met him only a few times while organizing the wedding of his father, Sir James Medway, but in that short time she'd discovered that he could talk the hind legs off a donkey and sell ice to an Eskimo.

Weddings were Gail's business. Over the last few years she'd built up Nuptia Creations, a firm that would take over every aspect of a wedding—the reception, the cake, the church, the music, the flowers, the groom's hired suit, the bridal gown and even the travel arrangements for the honeymoon. Usually it was the bride's family that called her in, but Liliane had no family, so her wealthy groom had told Gail to arrange everything—with the reception at his palatial country home, at his expense.

Sir James was a self-made man who'd started out with a market stall and finished with an industrial empire—and a knighthood. He was retired now, content to let his sons run Medway Industries while he basked in his past achievements and took innocent pride in his newly acquired title. Gail had found him kindly, generous to a fault and, despite his business acumen, slightly naive about every other aspect of the world. Perhaps he was a little naive about Liliane, his intended bride, but he was besotted by her and blissfully happy in a way Gail found touching.

They were standing in the huge morning room of Gracely Manor, the eighteenth-century mansion Sir James had bought with the fruits of his success. It stood in extensive grounds just outside the town of Chichley, ten miles from London. Chichley was a picturesque place, full of well-preserved old buildings, winding alleys and cobblestones. It looked just as an old English town ought to look, and in summer it attracted thousands of tourists.

It was only April now, but already the weather was summery. If Gail had been able to count on such weather she would have arranged the reception on the lawn. But, being unsure, she'd played it safe and held it indoors. The morning room was full of tables, each set out with the best crystal and silver and lavishly decorated with flowers. More tables, groaning with food, stood by the walls. This was the most deluxe wedding in Nuptia Creations's range, no expense spared. Everything was ready. But still the groom wouldn't give the signal to move.

A pretty young woman, dressed in a blue satin bridesmaid gown, appeared at Gail's side. This was Sylvia, Gail's cousin and also her assistant. As Liliane seemed to be bereft, not only of family but also of friends, Gail had had to supply bridesmaids also. This she'd done by hiring two resting actresses and co-opting Sylvia to lead them.

Their family resemblance was clear—both were tall and fair, but whereas Sylvia was gently pretty, Gail had something more. Her chin was small but firm and her looks were striking, almost to the point of beauty. Sylvia's gaze was lit by a sweet innocence that enchanted men because it made them think themselves fine fellows. Gail's expression was direct, with a hint of cool, appraising humor that could disconcert all but the most self-confident men.

Sylvia glided up to Gail now, her gown swirling about her ankles. "Miss Hatley wants to know why the holdup," she said.

"The holdup is the same as it's always been," Freddie said with a sigh. "Dad won't face the fact that Alex isn't coming."

"Oh dear, that's so sad."

"I'd better go up and smooth ruffled feathers," Gail declared briskly.

"My carnation's beginning to wilt," Freddie complained. He gave Sylvia his most winning smile. "Could you be very sweet and find me another?"

Watching the flush of pleasure come and go in Sylvia's face, Gail said with mock severity, "Nuptia Creations does *not* supply wilting flowers. There's nothing wrong with it."

"Well, I want another one, anyway," Freddie said irrepressibly.

Quick as a flash Sylvia found a fresh bloom and fixed it in Freddie's buttonhole, giving him a shy smile as she did so. She seemed to blush as she breathed, Gail thought, and the soft pink enhanced her delicate looks. She hoped Sylvia wasn't becoming smitten with Freddie, who was clearly a practiced flirt.

She found Sir James in his study, standing by the window that looked out over the front of the house. "You really ought to be going," she said gently.

He turned and his round face broke into a smile. "Oh yes—yes, of course. Mustn't keep the parson waiting, eh? It's just that—well, I thought..." His smile faded.

Damn Alex Medway! Gail thought furiously. How dare he be so cruel to this kindly man, who asked only for a little understanding on his big day!

A photograph had been placed in the center of the desk. It hadn't been so prominent when Gail had been in here a couple of days ago, but now it looked as though Sir James had been staring at it—when he wasn't staring over the empty drive. Gail studied it and saw a man in his thirties with a severe, unyielding face. He was good looking in a harsh sort of way, but her chief impression was that this wasn't a man to tangle with. There was no chance of affection making him relent.

"My son," Sir James said, following her gaze. "I did hope he'd be here, but he's very busy. He runs the whole firm now. Always off around the world making deals. He's in America this week—said he'd try to get back, but you know how it is—"

"It must be nice for you to know that your firm is in good hands," Gail said lamely.

"Yes—oh, yes. No man could have a better son. Not a better in the world." Sir James gave a sigh, as though finally giving up. "Well, I guess that's that. Will you tell Liliane that I'm going to start now?"

Gail went up to the luxurious bedroom which had been Liliane's since she moved into Gracely Manor three months ago. It was dominated by the huge double bed she shared with Sir James. Despite this, she'd insisted on being married in a virginal white gown, and Gail had to admit she looked a vision. "Whatever's happening?" she demanded. "Jamie should have left ages ago."

"He was hoping his son would manage to get here," Gail explained.

"He won't get here because he never meant to come," Liliane said crossly. "It's pure spite. When he couldn't stop the wedding he decided to spoil it. Poor Jamie will be so hurt."

"Well, he's about to leave for the church, and you can follow in ten minutes."

Liliane rose to her feet, and the crinoline gown of satin and lace swirled around her. She stood still while Gail adjusted her veil and smoothed down her skirts. "Perfect," Gail declared with satisfaction.

She went down to see Sir James into his car. As he was crossing the hall the bride began to descend. She gave a coy little scream when she saw him, hiding her face in her veil. "Go away!" she cried. "It's bad luck for you to see me before we meet in church."

"Come on, Dad," Freddie urged.

As Sir James went ahead to the car Gail realized that Freddie was smothering a grin. "What's so funny?" she demanded.

"Sorry, Gail. No disrespect to your excellent firm, but you've got to admit that all this flapdoodle has its funny side. Fancy telling him he mustn't see her yet, when they've been living together for three months! Mind you, she chucked him out to the spare room a week ago."

"People like to maintain the traditions at weddings," Gail informed him. "Where would I be if they didn't? Now, have you got the ring?"

"Yes ma'am. Here it is. Feels funny, being best man to your own father."

"Well, take good care of him."

A few moments later they were on their way. Now all Gail had to do was send the bride on after a suitable interval. But Liliane had decided to be temperamental. "I think I should keep him waiting just a little." She pouted. "It's the bride's privilege."

"Yes, but we're already running late," Gail said patiently, making a tiny adjustment to the veil. "I don't want to have any hitches."

Liliane laughed. "What kind of hitch? You don't think he'll get tired of waiting, do you?"

Gail smiled at this as she was obviously meant to. "You never know," she murmured abstractedly.

"Not my Jamie. No matter how late I am, he won't stand me up at the altar. Ouch! You tugged my hair."

"I'm sorry," Gail said quickly. "Is that better?"

"That's fine." Liliane gave Gail her most charming smile. "You've done such a lovely job with my wedding, Gail."

"Thank you."

"You must have seen so many brides. Did you ever know one who was really stood up at the altar?"

"Certainly none of mine have been," Gail said briskly. "I would consider it unprofessional to allow it to happen."

Liliane gave a ripple of laughter. "What a complete businesswoman you are. Do you see everything through a haze of figures?"

"It's safer that way," Gail said with a touch of dryness that was lost on Liliane, who was checking her appearance in the mirror. "Now you're ready to go."

At last the bride was sitting in the back of a limousine, next to the groom's brother, who was to give her away. The attendants piled into another car, and they were off. Gail breathed a sigh of relief. This wedding was proving trickier than most.

She went into the library and opened her laptop computer. While she waited for everyone to return she could get on with finalizing details for her next wedding. There were usually at least eight in the pipeline, at various stages of completion. Nuptia Creations was a huge success, which was ironic considering the events that had created it.

If David Cater hadn't been a spineless weakling, if his mother hadn't been a coldhearted bully and his father a well-meaning ditherer, then Gail wouldn't be sitting here this minute with the world at her feet and an emptiness in her heart.

She tried to slam a door on her thoughts, as she always did when they took this direction. That was all over. It had been over for years.

But her mind persisted in following Liliane to the church. She would be arriving about now. Sir James would turn to his bride with a smile on his face. There would be no betrayal for her, no spectators concealing their smirks behind their hands.

Liliane would leave the church on her new husband's arm, moving in stately glory, not fleeing humiliation with tears streaming down her face, as another bride had done, long ago....

Gail shut off the computer. It was no use. She couldn't work. She returned to the room where the reception was being held, meaning to calm herself by checking things that had been checked a dozen times already.

But she stopped in the doorway. A man was standing in front of the wedding cake. He had his back to her but the angle of his head and the set of his broad shoulders radiated cynicism as he regarded the five-tiered creation. "Excuse me—" she called.

He turned and she gasped when she saw who it was. "We weren't expecting you."

"We?" Alexander Medway raised his eyebrows. "Are you part of this three-ring circus?"

"I organized the wedding," she said stiffly.

"For money?"

"I'm being paid. Nuptia Creations is in the business of arranging weddings."

"A damned profitable business, if all this is anything to go by. How much did you squeeze out of my poor father?"

"Sir James said he wanted the best of everything."

"Yes, but how much?" he repeated grimly.

"I can't tell you that."

"You mean you haven't finished totting up the rich pickings?"

"No, I mean it's none of your business," Gail said sharply.

"*What?*" His tone was a mixture of anger and astonishment.

"My client is Sir James, not you, and I never betray a professional confidence."

His eyes were dark with anger. "Very neat."

Gail was in a fury now. Alexander Medway was tall and handsome, with an athletic build and a definite presence. But she was in no mood to consider his attractions. She'd seldom disliked anyone so much on so short an acquaintance. "You shouldn't be here," she said coldly.

"I didn't mean to come, but at the last minute I couldn't resist the circus."

"Well, I hope it doesn't disappoint you."

"Not at all. Everything is exactly as I'd expected—grandiose, overblown, triumphant."

"Triumphant?"

"I imagine Lily Hatch must feel a considerable sense of triumph at getting her hands on the Medway fortune."

"Who's Lily Hatch?"

"You know her as Liliane Hatley, but her name's Lily Hatch."

"You've been snooping on her," Gail said in disgust.

"I've had her thoroughly investigated, I don't deny it. It's what my father should have done."

"Your father is in love with her. How could you be so cruel as to spoil his big day? Don't you care about him at all?"

His eyes snapped with anger. "Now *you're* trespassing on ground that's none of your business. I have a great deal of affection for my father. That's why I've tried to save him from making a fool of himself."

"Perhaps he doesn't mind being a fool if he's a happy fool."

"Sentimental twaddle."

"When I said you shouldn't be here I meant you should be at the church. He wanted you to be his best man."

"That would have been more than I could stomach."

"Look, I haven't known your father very long, but it's been long enough for me to know that he's one of the kindest men I've ever met. I'll bet he's been a wonderful father to you."

Alex Medway sighed. "Is there some point to this?"

"The point is that you should forget your own feelings and think of him."

"I *have* been thinking of him. I've done everything I can to make him see sense."

At the words "see sense" Gail flinched as if someone had struck her. Alex Medway noticed and frowned, but before he could speak she recovered her poise and said, "If you had any decency you'd get right back in your car and drive to the church now. It would make his day."

"You really are a professional organizer, aren't you?" he snapped. "We're all just pawns on the wedding chessboard."

"Never mind that. Just do it. You know I'm right."

For a tense moment he scowled at her in silence. Then he strode to the door, but there he turned back. "What's your name?" he demanded.

"Gail Rivers."

"I'll remember it." He went out, leaving her with the feeling that she'd been noted down in his black book. She didn't care. He'd been noted down in *hers*.

But as her adrenaline subsided she found that she was shaking. It wasn't the brush with Alex Medway. She could cope with awkward characters. But this particular man had revived the very memories she had been trying to avoid, and given them a vividness that made her wretched all over again.

He was so like the members of that other family, the family she'd nearly married into. She'd loved David Cater with all the passion of eighteen, loved him with a completeness that blotted out everything else, including his wealth. She neither knew nor cared that he came from a rich family.

But she was soon made to care. The Caters were newly rich, anxious to consolidate their position by marrying their son to old money. They greeted the news of his engagement to penniless Gail Rivers with hostility. Mrs. Cater even tried to buy her off. Shocked, Gail had hotly refused.

Reluctantly the Caters had yielded to the inevitable, only stipulating that it should be a "proper" wedding, i.e., suitable to what they saw as their status. Gail, who had wanted only a quiet ceremony in a small country church, found herself swallowed up in elaborate preparations.

"Darling," she had pleaded, "I don't want a designer dress, or five hundred people at the reception, or enough champagne to sink a battleship or any of the other expensive things they're loading onto us."

David had smiled that easygoing smile that had made her heart turn over. "Why don't we just go along with what the family wants?" he'd asked. "At least they've agreed to the wedding."

Mrs. Cater appeared suddenly. Gail suspected she'd eavesdropped on the conversation, and was sure of it when the older woman took her aside later and said coldly, "Having wormed your way into this family, surely the least you can do is try to conform to its ways?''

"Wormed my way in?" Gail echoed, aghast. "Why, you can't even recognize love. Not even when it's for your own son."

"Love!" Mrs. Cater snorted. "You love his bank balance, all right! I wasn't taken in when you rejected cash, and I'm not taken in by your imitation of a shrinking violet now. You've got your eyes on bigger things. Considering your family, that's hardly surprising."

"There's nothing wrong with my family. Just because they don't have any money—"

Mrs. Cater had smiled her sweet, poisonous smile. "It's a little more than that, isn't it? I've had you investigated, young lady, and I know all about a certain relative of yours who just manages to stay out of prison by the skin of his teeth."

"I told David about Uncle Rex myself," Gail said, pale but proud. "And he doesn't care."

"To be sure, you got your word in first. Very clever. Oh, how can my son be such a fool as not to see through you?"

"David's in love with me," Gail said confidently. "And I'm in love with him."

Mrs. Cater didn't seem to think this worth answering. She merely eyed Gail with dislike and walked away.

The wedding day was burned into her memory so deeply that neither time nor effort could eradicate it: the long, black limousine arriving for her, the sudden realization that she was beautiful in her fairy-tale white dress, her eyes alight with love and the conviction that she would make her marriage work because love conquers all.

But David hadn't been at the church. With cruel spite, his mother had waited until the last minute to tell her, had let her get out of the car and come as far as the aisle, where she could be seen by all the guests. And then, in the sight of them all, she'd said simply that the groom would not be putting in an appearance.

"David came to his senses just in time."

At first Gail simply hadn't understood. It was several moments before she realized that David had left the church a few minutes earlier in response to his mother's frantic pleas, and was actually on his way to the airport for a holiday "To recover from the strain."

"David came to his senses just in time."

She'd looked around at the crowd of richly dressed people, all studying her with interest. And a cry broke from her as she dropped her bouquet to cover her face with her hands. The next moment she was fleeing the church, tearing off the gorgeous lace veil and leaving it on the ground, tears streaming down her face as she fled in a vain attempt to escape the brutal truth.

They'd won. In the end, the rich, cruel Caters had won.

Eventually she'd accepted the fact that she'd been mistaken about David. A man worth having would never have simply abandoned her in such a spineless way. She never heard from him again—not a letter, not a phone call. He left it all to his parents.

Her scorn for him revived her courage and imbued her heart with defiance. When an embarrassed Mr. Cater sent her a generous check in "compensation" she resisted the impulse to tear it up. Instead she banked it the same day.

The one good thing to come out of the mess was her friendship with Miss Littleham, the professional wedding organizer who'd arranged everything. She went to work for her and became so good at the job that eventually she took over as manager. In due course she used the Cater check to buy in as partner. Under her cool efficiency and imaginative marketing techniques the sedate, old-fashioned little firm was transformed into a thriving modern business. Profits leapt until, on Miss Littleham's retirement, Gail was able to buy her out completely.

The little brown mouse had vanished. Gail had built on her devastating experience to turn herself into an elegant, supremely successful entrepreneur, running the best firm of its kind for miles around. She now employed a secretary plus four assistants. People came to Nuptia Creations first, begging her to find a space for them on her crowded books, and several clients had postponed their weddings as the only way of securing her services.

On the face of it, there was nothing to connect her with the shy girl who'd fled the church in tears. But inside the prosperous, sophisticated woman, that girl still lived in a place that Gail guarded carefully from intruders.

Then Alex Medway had come crashing in with his callous assumptions and his brutal insistence on thinking the worst. And it was as if the Caters were there again, cold, domineering, determined to crush opposition and make everyone "see sense." Their kind of sense.

Gail walked about restlessly, wishing that the bridal party would return soon and save her from being alone with her thoughts. But of course, Alex Medway would also be returning.

A waiter from the catering company she'd hired was hovering in readiness. "Can I get you a drink before the ravenous hordes arrive?" he asked. "You look as if you need one."

"I think I do."

"A nice glass of chilled champagne?"

Gail gave a mirthless little laugh. "No champagne, thank you," she said. "Anything but champagne."

Chapter Two

At last the first limousine appeared around the bend in the drive and glided slowly to a halt outside the front door. Sir James and the new Lady Medway stepped out and entered the house together. The groom was beaming with joy and continually gave his bride glances of fond pride. The other cars disgorged bridesmaids and guests and soon the reception room was full to overflowing with well-dressed, chattering people.

Sir James noticed Gail and pounced eagerly. "Guess what?" he exclaimed. "Alex came after all. He arrived at the church, right in the middle of the service. What do you think of that?"

"Well, you were always sure he wouldn't let you down," Gail said, smiling at him warmly.

"Exactly. I said he'd do his best to get here and none of you believed me."

Gail became aware that Alex had joined the edge of the group and was looking uncomfortable under his father's praise. She met his eyes, and the way he colored gave her an angry satisfaction. At least he had the grace to be ashamed.

The guests were studying the seating plan to find where they'd been put. Sir James led his bride to the top table, followed by Freddie and the bridesmaids. Alex found his own name by a place setting near his father, and glanced up at Gail. "Did you have to do much juggling to put me here?" he asked.

"None. That place was always reserved for you. I told you, your father *knew* you'd come."

"I didn't know myself until a couple of hours ago."

"Perhaps he understands you better than you think. He talks as if you possess all the virtues. Do you?"

"One or two," he said dryly. "None of the agreeable ones."

"That's what I thought."

He flashed her a sharp glance. "Where will you be sitting?" he demanded.

"Nowhere. I have duties to attend to." She moved away quickly, leaving Alex staring after her, his mouth grim and his eyes baffled.

Soon everyone was seated for the meal. Gail glided about, keeping a close eye on everything. She sought out Sylvia, and checked with her that all had gone well in the church. "And how come you're sitting here?" she asked. "I put you three places along."

"I did it," Freddie said instantly, from the next seat. "Mea culpa." He beat his breast, not sounding in the least penitent. "Best man's privilege to bag the prettiest bridesmaid."

Sylvia touched a sapphire pendant about her neck. "Isn't this lovely?" she asked. "Sir James gave one to all the bridesmaids."

"You ought to be covered in jewels," Freddie said gallantly, and Sylvia smiled shyly.

Gail straightened up and found Alex Medway regarding this little scene, evidently having overheard everything. She met his gaze, then turned away, hoping he'd continue on his best behavior for his father's sake. Something about his cynical expression made her fear the worst.

But she had a shock when the toasts began. Freddie, as best man, made a short speech, but then Alex rose unexpectedly. A buzz ran around the crowd—everyone knew the story of his late arrival, and his disapproval of the wedding. But now he was smiling, although rather pale.

"You all thought I wouldn't make it, didn't you?" he asked with a grin. "But I did make it, because nothing would have kept me away from this occasion. Since my mother died, my brother and I know how lonely Dad's been, and we've hoped that he could be happy again. Those who are fond of my father—and that means everyone who knows him—will be glad to drink to him—and his wife—today." He raised his champagne glass and a forest of glasses was raised in response.

Sir James was beaming. The new Lady Medway looked pleased. But Alex looked beyond them to where Gail stood, astonished, he was glad to see.

His thoughts were disorganized, something that he disliked because he wasn't used to it. He was furious with her for dictating to him about going to the church, and annoyed with himself for yielding. But he'd been startled and moved at the joy that flooded his father's face when he appeared. It showed him what a cruel act he'd nearly committed, and he knew he owed Gail a debt of gratitude. But knowing it was one thing, admitting it quite another. His proud, unyielding nature felt the situation as gall and wormwood.

He'd delivered the speech to please his father and also because he needed to stand well in his own opinion. Making that annoying woman realize that she didn't know everything had been a remote consideration—if, indeed, he'd thought of it at all.

At last it was time for the dancing. Waiters cleared the tables and pushed them closer to the wall. The orchestra struck up and Sir James took the floor with his bride, proving himself a surprisingly good dancer for so plump a man. Alex led the applause as they did the first circuit alone. Freddie promptly claimed Sylvia for a dance, and Gail went to have a word with the headwaiter.

"Come along," Sir James called out to her as he flew nimbly past with Liliane. "You should be dancing."

"I'm here to work," Gail protested with a laugh.

"Nonsense. Enjoy yourself. Alex, make her stop working."

Alex came to her side. "You heard what my father said."

"There's no need for you to dance with me," she said briskly.

"But there is. It's what Dad wants, and nothing must spoil his big day. Your own words."

"I was talking about serious things, not a whim."

"Dad's whims are important to him. That's how he got successful, by never letting go. Look, he's watching us."

"In that case, we mustn't disappoint him," she said coolly.

To her surprise Alex was, like his father, an excellent dancer. Once on the floor the ramrod stiffness seemed to fall away from his body, and he performed the steps with a sensuous ease that inspired a response in her. It had been a long day and Gail was full of tension, but now she found her limbs loosening as he guided her through the dance. She disliked Alex Medway, but he was a pleasure to dance with.

The music switched to a waltz and he drew her close. Again she sensed the fluidity with which he blended his movements with the music, as though dancing gave him a much needed release. But as Gail felt his hand firm in the small of her back, and the touch of his thighs as they briefly brushed her own, she knew this dance was a mistake. Close up, she recognized that there was another Alex Medway than the hard, stubborn man who'd almost broken his father's heart. This other man had a strong, athletic body that spoke of lusty appetites and frequent gratification. To Gail, who had determinedly quelled both appetites and emotions within herself, his nearness was a strain.

She ventured to glance up and found his mouth very close. Now that it was relaxed it had a sensual curve that suggested a great deal about his nature. She became aware that the room was warmer than she'd thought, and wished she was dressed for dancing, in a low-cut gown, instead of wearing her severely elegant business suit.

"That was a very nice speech you made," she said, for the sake of something to say.

"I wish you could have seen your face," he replied. "It was so obvious that you were expecting the worst of me. Despite what you think, I'm very fond of my father. It's done now. I tried to stop it and failed. End of subject. You're an excellent dancer."

"So are you," she returned, accepting his desire to change the subject. "But I shouldn't be doing this. I'm not dressed for dancing."

"True. You should be wearing a long black dress, made of something clinging," he said, as if considering the matter seriously.

"I don't think that would suit me at all."

"You don't know what would suit you," he said arrogantly. "I do. I'd like to see you in that dress."

"Well, you never will," she said, nettled by his tone. "After today we won't meet again."

A slight smile touched his mouth. "I wouldn't be surprised if you were wrong about that."

"I would," she said firmly. "Very surprised."

"How often will you find a dancing partner who's as right for you as I am?"

"Does it matter? I hardly ever dance—"

"You should dance more often. With me."

He was impossible. She relapsed into silence. After a moment she looked up to find him regarding her with a humorous look that transformed his face. She smiled in response and they laughed together. "That's better," he said. "You're much too controlled. I wonder why?"

"I'm surprised at you for having such a vivid imagination, Mr. Medway," she said primly.

"I have no imagination at all, but I know what I see. You're an interesting woman, all coolness and rigidity on the surface and fire inside."

"You don't know what's inside," she said with a sudden flare of temper.

"But I do. I can feel it when you dance against me."

"Please don't hold me so close. People are looking at us."

"They're looking because we move so well together. Let's give them something to look at."

The music was changing to a rumba. Before Gail could pull out of his arms, Alex had drawn her irresistibly into a series of intricate steps. It took all Gail's concentration to follow him. She wondered if she was mad. He was a stranger, and one that she disliked. Yet here she was, doing the rumba—a dance that called on the protagonists to appear joined at the hip—with *him* of all men. Then a strange thing happened. As her hips moved in perfect unison with his, she found that anxiety fell away to be replaced by exhilaration. Her whole body seemed to be singing with joy.

What she was doing felt right and natural. The music flowed through his body and hers, uniting them as if they'd been made for each other. She knew her movements had developed a sensuous wriggle that was new to her, but there was nothing she could do about it. Some magic power had taken control, lifting her outside herself, making her do things she wouldn't normally dream of, making her glory in them. And that power was called Alex Medway.

The end came with a long, sensuous note on the trumpet. Alex pressed her gently backward against the crook of his arm, and she followed his guidance, knowing she was in the hands of a master. The next moment she was lying back against his arm in an attitude of abandon, while he leaned over her, gazing down into her face, his eyes hooded and sensual. A look like that should be a prelude to a kiss. Her heart was beating wildly.

A burst of applause brought her back to reality. For the first time, she realized that they were the only couple dancing. The others had drawn back into a circle, admiring them. Alex helped to draw her upright, and she saw on his face the same startled amazement that she knew must be on her own. She wondered if she'd been making an exhibition of herself, but she didn't care. Her blood was still dancing.

"The next time we do that, you'll be wearing a black, clinging dress," Alex said in a slightly ragged voice.

"But we—I'm not sure—" She had to get away from his dominant presence, right this minute. "I have to help the bride get ready to leave," she said breathlessly. "Excuse me."

She almost ran from the dance floor, following Sylvia and Liliane up the stairs. The bride had to divest herself of her wedding gown, and Gail was glad to have work to do. It would help her banish the memory of whirling in Alex Medway's arms, and the message in his eyes.

At last Liliane was arrayed in her traveling clothes. Her luggage was already piled in the car outside. "You look gorgeous," Sylvia said sincerely.

"Are you sure I haven't forgotten anything?" Liliane asked.

"Only your bouquet," Gail said. "You should have tossed it as you came upstairs."

"Well, I'll take it down again and throw it as I leave."

There was a knock on the door, and Sir James called, "Are you ready, darling?"

The guests cheered as they went outside together. Amid a chorus of "Goodbye—good luck," Sir James seized his bride by the hand and ran with her down the steps to where the chauffeur was standing by the open door of the car. Liliane paused a moment before getting in, and sent her bouquet sailing in an arc over everyone's head to where Gail and Sylvia stood together.

Gail tried to step aside and let the prize go to Sylvia, but Alex had appeared at her elbow and she couldn't move past him. Before she knew it she was holding the bouquet.

A frisson ran through her. Then she pulled herself together, forced a smile and tossed the flowers to Sylvia. "Oh, no. They're for you," her cousin protested, laughing.

"Not me," Gail said, turning away before Sylvia could do anything.

Alex took her arm as they returned inside. "Where is the happy couple going to?"

"The honeymoon is a Caribbean cruise." She looked at him significantly, waiting for a cynical comment.

He read her look and shrugged. "I have no more to say—at least, not until she shows herself in her true colors."

"If she makes your father happy, surely that's all that matters?"

"But for how long? I give it three months. By then he'll have seen through her and thrown her out. She'll be negotiating for a huge payoff, and I shall personally make sure she doesn't get one."

"Perhaps he won't throw her out. You can't make his decisions for him. But I guess you're used to telling people what to do."

"It's my job," he said with a look of surprise.

"Well, you're not at work now."

"But *you* are, aren't you? I dare say, you're doing very well out of all this."

The magic that had united them as they danced had fallen away, leaving their original antagonism as bright and sharp as before. "If you're trying to be offensive, Mr. Medway, you're succeeding," Gail said crisply.

"I'm a good saleswoman but I never sell people more than they can afford."

"And my father can afford a great deal."

"Don't you ever think about anything except money?"

"Not often. I can't afford to. The trouble with having money, is the number of people trying to take it away."

"I see. Your real objection to Liliane is that she'll take some of your inheritance?"

He frowned. "Now it's your turn to be offensive."

"I thought it was a fair comment. You're determined to think the worst of other people's motives. Why should you be surprised when somebody thinks the worst of yours? Your trouble, Mr. Medway, is that you can dish it out, but you can't take it. Now, perhaps you'll excuse me. As you pointed out, I'm working."

She left him quickly. She had a sense of relief at putting a distance between them. There was a dangerous animal vitality about him that set her blood racing, and she didn't like it. It felt too much like the feelings that had afflicted her with David, and she was determined never to experience those again.

She went to have a word with the orchestra conductor about a booking she'd given him for a wedding the following week. When they'd finished talking, and he lifted his baton again, she found Alex waiting for her. "I apologize," he said.

"So do I. I shouldn't have said all that. It was a cheap shot."

"And quite untrue. I already own a fair chunk of Medway Industries. The old man signed part of it over to me when I took charge. I admit that I don't relish Lily Hatch getting her elegant claws into any of the rest, but that isn't for mercenary reasons. The most valuable thing my father has bequeathed me is his business savvy, and nobody can take that away. I'll survive whatever happens. Freddie's another matter."

"He seems bright enough."

"He—to put it mildly—is impressionable. I've found a niche for him in selling, where he's quite good and can't do much harm."

"*You've* found a niche for him?" she echoed. "That's pretty patronizing, isn't it?"

"He needs looking after. I'm looking after him, the way I've always done. What's patronizing about that?"

"He's a grown man."

"He's a playful puppy who needs watching in case he gets too near the fire." His eyes fixed on Freddie, whirling by in the direction of the French doors, with Sylvia in his arms. "Speaking of which, who's that bridesmaid he keeps dancing with?"

"For heavens sake!" Gail exclaimed, exasperated. "Let him at least choose his own dancing partner."

"Since he's taking her out on the terrace I think he has more than dancing on his mind."

"Surely that's his choice, too, isn't it?"

"Not with one of rapacious Lily's friends it isn't."

"Well, you're quite wrong," Gail said, her temper rising. "She's actually my cou—"

"Just a moment," Alex interrupted her and turned away in pursuit of Freddie. Gail caught up with him.

"You can't go out and disturb him now."

"Watch me!" He strode out onto the terrace. Gail followed, fuming.

Freddie and Sylvia were sitting on the stone balustrade. He held her hand between his, in a gesture that struck Gail as touchingly old-fashioned. But Alex didn't appear to be touched. He coughed in a way that made Freddie look up and Sylvia withdraw her hand quickly. "You've got a knack for turning up at the wrong moment, older brother," Freddie said with a wry look.

"Evidently. And you have a genius for forgetting your obligations," Alex told him. "Now Dad's gone, you're the host, and you shouldn't leave your guests."

Freddie grinned. "They've got *you*. They don't need me."

"But you live in this house and I don't," Alex said smoothly. "That makes you the one in charge."

"I don't recall hearing myself described as being in charge before," Freddie said in a grumble. "Usually it's 'Freddie, do this,' or 'Freddie, get moving.'"

"Get moving, now," Alex told him firmly.

Freddie looked belligerent, but Sylvia put a gentle hand on his arm. "Your brother's right," she said. "I shouldn't be taking up so much of your time."

"You can have all of my time, whenever you want it," Freddie said defiantly. To underline his point he placed a swift kiss on her mouth before departing, and held her hand firmly in his, so that she had no choice but to go with him.

"Talk about a tyrant!" Gail snapped.

"One fortune hunter is enough in this family," Alex retorted. "I don't want another one trapping my brother."

"How dare you call Sylvia a fortune hunter!"

"She was very interested in that sapphire pendant."

"That doesn't mean—"

"And she's a friend of Lily's. That fact alone sets my antennae at 'Danger'!"

"Well, for once your antennae have failed you," Gail informed him furiously. "Far from being friends, they'd never met until this morning. We needed an extra bridesmaid so I called in Sylvia, who happens to be my cousin."

She had the pleasure of seeing him taken aback, and the even grater pleasure of realizing how much he hated being caught off guard. "All right," he said at last. "I didn't mean to insult your cousin—"

"You don't care who you insult, as long as you get your own way."

Alex didn't answer at first. He took a long breath and seemed to be struggling for words. "We have a problem," he said at last.

"You bet we do!"

"I mean the fact that we react to each other in two opposite ways."

"Not true. I only react to you in one way, with dislike."

"You're overlooking what happened to us on the dance floor."

She shrugged. "A dance! So what?"

"So this," he said quietly, and took hold of her.

She was in his arms before she could resist, her gasp of anger smothered by his mouth covering hers. The touch of his lips went through her like fire. It was like being back on the dance floor—her body attuned to his, asking no more than for that thrilling union to last. But the self-assurance with which he claimed her roused her antagonism, and she freed herself with a firm push. "You had no right to do that," she said breathlessly.

He was watching her face closely. "I believe in shortcuts. We got off on the wrong foot, but underneath—we want each other."

"You're deluding yourself."

"I'm a man who makes decisions quickly. I know what I want at once, and I want you. If I rushed you a bit, I'm sorry. Maybe you need more time, but the result will be the same."

His unmatched arrogance left her speechless, but at last she managed to say, "Mr. Medway, please try to believe that I dislike you more than anyone I've ever known—"

"I thought we'd covered that ground," he said impatiently. "There's something between us, whether we like it or not."

"And I gather you don't like it?" she snapped.

"Well, do *you?* As far as I'm concerned you're part of the system that's helping a cheap little gold digger make a fool of my father. You compound that crime by ordering me about in my own home, and I actually let you get away with it. I don't like anything about this whole situation, but for some reason or other you've got under my skin. I want you. I want you in my life, my arms and my bed. I can't put it plainer than that. I won't let you make a fool of me, but anything else is yours for the asking."

Gail stared at him, unable to believe that she'd heard correctly. "And just what, exactly, do you count as making a fool of you?" she asked when she could speak.

"I'm a skilled campaigner. I offer the best—an apartment, jewels, a gold credit card—whatever your heart desires. Everything but marriage."

"And do you seriously believe my heart would ever desire marriage with you? You flatter yourself."

"I'm flattering *you* with the assumption that you're a sensible woman who knows a good thing when she sees one."

"A good thing?" she repeated with cynical hilarity. "You? A man with a mind like a cash box?"

"Plenty of people have minds like cash boxes," Alex said coolly. "I just happen to possess a key, which I'm offering you—for a while."

"There isn't enough money in the world to tempt me," she said witheringly.

"Come on. Surely it's better than working for your living? I'm sure your boss is paying you good commission on the weddings you sell, but is it really worth the long hours?"

"You know nothing about me, or my life."

"I know one thing about you. There's something deep inside you that's ready to be mine. I know it because I feel the same. Nobody feels that way unless it's mutual, so why don't you drop the coy maneuvering and give me a straight answer?"

"I've already given you one, but you're too conceited to hear," she told him angrily. "Shall I shout it to get it through your thick skull?"

He shook his head and his eyes gleamed wickedly. "You'll get through to me much better like this," he said, drawing her firmly into his arms.

"I've told you I'm *not*—" Her words were smothered by the pressure of his mouth over hers.

Fury at his self-assurance surged up within her, making her hot blood pound through her veins. She tried to push him away, but he was holding her tightly. This was a man of supreme confidence, who had no doubts about himself or his ability to get what he wanted. But if he thought he was simply going to overcome her, he had another think coming. She stopped struggling and went still in his arms, refusing to move a muscle.

After a moment, he stopped and looked down at her flushed, angry face. "Passive resistance," he murmured with a hint of humor. "I like that. It shows subtlety."

"You unspeakable—"

"But I can be subtle too," he interrupted. He dropped his head and caressed her neck, just below one ear, with lips that teased. "Don't stop," he murmured. "Go on telling me how unspeakable and appalling I am. I can listen at the same time."

"You've got a nerve," she whispered distractedly. "Let me go at once. How dare you act as if . . . aaah." Her words faded into a gasp as the tip of his tongue flickered against her neck. The shivers of delight that scurried through her made her dizzy. She clung onto something for dear life, and found too late that what she was clinging to was him.

He was actually daring to laugh, she realized. She could feel his laughter vibrating through her from the contact of his burning lips. "But I always act 'as if,'" he murmured. "It's the quickest way to make 'as if' reality."

"And you think you can just roll over me like a juggernaut?" she demanded in a shaking voice.

"Well, I'm not doing too badly now, am I?" he whispered, moving around so that his lips were tracing the line of her jaw. To her dismay, this was even more shattering. The line of pleasure seemed to run down her neck, over her breasts, right down to her loins. He was doing exactly what he wanted to, leaving her helpless in the grip of unexpected desire.

"You burn me up," he murmured. "Don't tell me it isn't the same with you. What are you waiting for?"

Instead of giving her a chance to reply he covered her mouth with his own, tightening his arms to draw her hard against him. Gail's head was swimming, and when she felt his tongue slide between her teeth she had no power to resist him. Warmth was stealing over her, possessing her. She hadn't known that her body could ignite so quickly, and now the discovery was thrilling and terrifying. She didn't feel like herself. She felt like another woman, who only wanted to be in Alex Medway's arms.

That other woman put her arms about him as though she craved him more than anything in the world. She opened her mouth and felt a rush of joy at the intensity of his exploration. She wanted more. She wanted everything. She'd shut herself off from passion, imprisoning her inner self behind doors that were bolted and barred. But now he'd come storming in, flinging the doors wide open and tossing aside her defenses with his imperious certainty that she would do as he wished. And she was meekly doing it. What was worse, she gloried in it. The feel of his taut, muscular body pressed hard against hers, thrilled her with its latent promise.

He was speaking again, kissing her face all over. "Be honest, Gail. Doesn't my proposition seem a little more attractive now?"

"Wh-what?"

"Are you ready to take a practical view—or shall we try a little more persuasion?"

His smile as he murmured the soft words, and a certain something in his voice that plainly said he was sure of victory, pierced her consciousness like a sliver of ice, extinguishing the passion that only a moment ago had roared almost out of control. Suddenly the "other" woman was banished and Gail was herself again, furious with him *and* herself for being such a fool. "There's no need," she said in a voice that should have warned him. "I've made my decision."

"Good." His lips were over hers again. "Why don't you just show me—?"

Putting out all her strength she pushed him away. "I've made my decision, and it's *no,*" she said firmly.

He was still holding her, enough to feel the trembling of her slim body. Perhaps that was why he made his big mistake. "I don't think you mean that," he said. "Your lips say no, but your kisses tell me yes."

He tried to draw her close again. With a sudden explosion of temper, Gail thrust him off her and gave him a stinging slap across the face. "Now there'll be no misunderstanding," she snapped.

Turning, she ran swiftly down the steps of the terrace and didn't stop running until she'd reached her car. She drove away without looking back, so she didn't see him holding his face and staring after her, thunderstruck.

Chapter Three

Gail knew what she was about to hear as soon as she arrived at work and found Sylvia waiting for her, her eyes shining. "Oh, Gail," Sylvia cried, "I'm engaged. Freddie asked me last night, and I said yes."

Gail forced herself to smile. "That's wonderful, darling!" she exclaimed. But her words were only a cover for her misgivings.

For three months, ever since the Medway wedding, she'd dreaded this moment. She knew about every date Sylvia had had with Freddie, because her young cousin had always been bubbling over the next morning. She'd watched with dismay as Sylvia had fallen under Freddie's spell, trying not to see in her a reincarnation of herself, years ago. She'd told herself she was being paranoid, had prayed Sylvia's feelings would die a natural, painless death, yet all in vain. Sylvia was wildly, passionately in love, with all its possibilities for terrible hurt.

"Are you really pleased for me?" Sylvia begged. "I know you don't like Freddie much but—"

"Whatever makes you think that? Of course I like Freddie. I think he's charming."

"Well, you've always warned me not to get too involved with him. You said charm was all very well, but it couldn't be relied on."

"Did I?" Gail stared. She'd been thinking these things, but she hadn't realized that she'd said them quite as often as Sylvia implied. "I didn't mean to sound like a killjoy, and I do like Freddie. It's just—"

"You're thinking of David, aren't you? But Freddie isn't like that. Honestly."

"Nobody knows what people are like until they're put under pressure," Gail said. "I never saw that side of David until he cracked under pressure from his family."

"But Freddie's family is fine. He took me home last night to tell them we're engaged, and Sir James is thrilled."

"What did Lady Medway say?"

"She wasn't there. She's spending a few days in London, buying new clothes."

"She never seems to be around," Gail said thoughtfully. In the last few weeks, since the Medways had returned from their honeymoon, whenever Freddie had taken Sylvia home it seemed that Lady Medway was usually away on a shopping trip. Sir James, according to Sylvia, was as besotted by her as ever, but a puzzled look was creeping into his eyes.

"And Alex?" Gail asked now. "Was he thrilled?"

"I don't know. He doesn't live at Gracely Manor. They keep a room for him, but he has an apartment in

London, and right now he's abroad on business. But why should he mind?"

"He has—funny ideas," Gail said vaguely. "Remember how hard he tried to stop his father's wedding? He's suspicious of everyone who wants to marry into that family."

"Don't you like Alex?" Sylvia asked.

"I dislike him intensely."

"That's odd."

"There's nothing odd about it. I should think everyone who knows him must dislike him."

"But I got the feeling that you—that you and he—I mean, when you did the rumba together—Freddie said that when people did the rumba as perfectly in tune as you and Alex, it meant that what they really wanted was to be—well, doing something else," Sylvia said lamely, for Gail's frosty eyes were upon her.

"Freddie has a vivid imagination, and you should advise him to keep it under control."

"Yes, Gail," Sylvia said meekly.

"And he can keep his tongue under control as well."

"Yes, Gail." Sylvia's tone was still meek but her eyes were mischievous. "So you don't want to know the other thing Freddie said?"

"I imagine you're going to tell me."

"He said Alex always gets what he wants, just like Sir James."

"That hardly concerns me, since Alex Medway and I most certainly do not want each other."

"That's not what Freddie s—"

"Sylvia, if you tell me again what Freddie said I shall get cross," Gail said desperately.

"All right, then I won't say it. But Sir James wants me to take you to dinner tonight. You can make it, can't you?"

"Of course I can make it."

"And Freddie's going to buy me a ring this lunch-time, so can I—?"

"Yes, you can take a long lunch hour."

Not for the world would Gail have spoiled Sylvia's pleasure, or let her suspect the other reason why this wedding dismayed her. It would bring her back into contact with Alex Medway, and that was the last thing in the world she wanted.

She found it hard to concentrate on her work for the rest of the day. It had taken three months to drive Alex out of her thoughts and the battle had exhausted her. At any moment a stray snatch of music on the radio might send memory flooding through her limbs, making them long to move again in the perfect rhythm they shared with Alex.

She hadn't seen or heard from him since the moment she'd slapped his face and stormed out, but the feeling of his lips on her own had lingered, torturing her as she lay awake in the small hours.

What troubled her even more was the memory of her own reaction, the shameless way she'd melted in his arms. The defenses she'd thought so impregnable had melted to nothing before his onslaught. It was only his arrogance that had saved her from yielding further to a man she disliked, but who had the mysterious power to make her blood sing in her veins.

At last her common sense came to her rescue. The whole thing could be explained by the way he'd taken her by surprise. If she met him again she'd be on her guard, and nothing would happen. Just the same, she would prefer *not* to meet him again.

At midday Sylvia hurried off and returned two hours later with a glittering diamond ring on her left hand. "It's much bigger than I wanted," she confided, "but Freddie was so keen to buy this one that I couldn't bear to disappoint him."

She was aglow with happiness. Looking at her, Gail uttered a silent prayer that Sylvia at least might see her dreams come true.

Although it was high summer, the weather had hit an uncertain patch, and near the end of the afternoon the heavens opened. By the time they left for Gracely Manor a full-scale thunderstorm had developed. Gail drove slowly, while the wipers of her car fought to keep up with the heavy rain. When they were nearly at their destination Gail asked, as casually as she could, "Have you told Freddie anything about your father?"

"Only that he used to be a clerk in a factory, and now he's unemployed."

"Nothing else?"

"You mean about . . . ?" Sylvia left the implication hanging in the air.

Sylvia's father was the "uncle Rex" that David Cater's mother had found so unacceptable. He was an amiable man with an unfortunate weakness. He couldn't resist gambling, and he always lost. At last he'd helped himself to his firm's funds, and was almost immediately caught. His family rallied around to replace the money and there was no prosecution, but he lost his job and thereafter was on a slippery slope down. For the last few years he'd lived on the edge of the law.

As she became more successful, Gail had stepped in several times to bail him out, but he began to take her help for granted. At last she'd had to stand firm against his demands or risk being dragged down as well. He'd tried petty theft, been caught, charged and found guilty and given a suspended sentence.

It was a story that Alex was bound to uncover, Gail thought grimly, and it would make him think the worst. "Have you told Freddie?" she asked again.

"Well, no—I didn't think of it. I've been so happy I forgot everything else. Do you think I should tell him?"

Gail nodded emphatically. "If I were you I should get your word in before Alex Medway does."

As they drew up outside the house Sylvia exclaimed, "Oh look, there's Lady Medway at the window. I'm sure Sir James said she wasn't due back until the end of the week."

"I expect she returned in your honor," Gail said. But she could make out Liliane's expression, and it wasn't one of pleasure.

Sir James welcomed them both with open arms. Liliane received them graciously but with reserve, almost, Gail thought, as though she'd never met them before. She was fashionably dressed, exquisitely groomed and looked as if she'd lived in elegant surroundings all her life.

"It's so nice to meet you again," she said politely. "The maid will bring us some sherry directly." A maid entered, bearing a tray with glasses. She wore a traditional black uniform with a white apron and cap. "We'll have them over here," Lady Medway said.

"Yes, your ladyship."

Gail stared. When she'd been here last, the servants had worn normal clothing and spoken to Sir James in a chatty, informal way that he seemed to like. Evidently the new Lady Medway had been making changes.

"Well, let's see the ring!" Sir James insisted. He took the hand that Sylvia shyly held out, exclaimed with pleasure and drew Liliane forward to look.

"Beautiful," Lady Medway said with a cool smile. "But are you wise to be so extravagant, Freddie? You'll have plenty of other things to buy for the wedding."

Sir James and his son exchanged a quick glance and Gail was suddenly convinced that it was he, not Freddie, who was paying for the ring. Liliane seemed to have realized it, too, for she frowned and gave a quick glance at her own engagement ring. It outshone Sylvia's, but only just. To Gail it was as though the air about her had vibrated with tension, but she was sure Sylvia noticed nothing.

"Well, shall we go in and eat?" Sir James asked jovially.

"Not yet, darling," Liliane admonished him gently. "The maid hasn't announced it yet."

"Oh—oh, yes." Sir James looked like a chastened little boy.

At that moment the uniformed maid appeared and intoned, "Dinner is served, my lady."

"Jolly good!" Sir James said enthusiastically, which made his wife give him a little frown.

"Now, you must take Sylvia in," Liliane insisted, "as she's the guest of honor—"

"Why don't we just all go in together?" Freddie said quickly. As he moved into the dining room at Gail's side he muttered, "It's like this *all* the time, heaven help us!"

Over dinner Sir James dropped his bombshell. "As soon as Freddie told me he was engaged to Sylvia, I said nobody but you must arrange the wedding," he told Gail jovially. "I want exactly what Liliane and I had—

everything of the best, at my expense, of course. No, no, my dear, I insist," he added to Sylvia, who'd made a sound of protest. "I always wanted a daughter and now I'm going to have one. And she's going to be welcomed into this family with a bang."

"But truly, I don't need a lavish affair," Sylvia pleaded. She was forced to stop as a crack of thunder overhead drowned her out. When the noise had faded she said, "Just a quiet ceremony and a small reception, with a few friends—"

"I think that would be most suitable," Liliane interrupted. She laid a gentle hand on Sir James's arm. "You shouldn't overwhelm poor Sylvia with a big display that she doesn't want, darling. In fact, I can't see any need to rush the wedding at all. They're both so young. Marriage is a big step. It needs thinking about."

It dawned on Gail that Liliane was hostile to this marriage. Like a cat, she hid her claws deep within silky fur, but they could still be glimpsed. Why? Gail wondered. What did Liliane have against Sylvia?

Sir James seemed oblivious to these undertones. "Nonsense," he declared heartily. "Once you've made your mind up, the sooner the better, I say. We'll have it just as we did before, only bigger and better. I'm not having anyone say we splashed out on our own wedding and skimped on Freddie's." He beamed at Sylvia. "It would look as if we didn't want you in the family, my dear, and we can't have that."

Against this kindly onslaught Sylvia retreated, and Sir James was left to rumble on like a genial juggernaut. Gail tried to halt him. "Sir James—"

"Jimmy. We're all family now," he said.

"Jimmy, I'm not sure that it's a good idea for me to organize the wedding," she said desperately.

"Nonsense. It has to be you. I've been looking over the figures..." He produced a notebook that Gail recognized as the one he'd used to make notes when discussing his own wedding with her.

"Surely this could wait until later?" Liliane asked in a chill, tinkly voice.

"You're right," Sir James said. "We'll..." He stopped and raised his voice against the din of the rain lashing the windowpanes. "We'll talk over coffee. My goodness, I pity anyone out in this weather!"

Gail sat trying to think of some way out of this, but nothing occurred to her. She should have anticipated it, she realized, but she hadn't. Now she was faced with the prospect of coming into continual contact with Alex Medway, and she would prefer anything to that, she told herself.

As they made their way into the library for coffee she drew Freddie aside. "Have you told your brother, yet?" she asked.

"In a way."

"What does that mean?"

"I couldn't get him on the phone so I left a message on his answering machine. No doubt his secretary will collect it and pass it on when she's got the 'serious matters' out of the way first. Actually, it's going to be a bit awkward when he gets back because Liliane took a fancy to—"

"Come on, you two," Sir James called. "We've got a little ceremony to perform."

"I'll tell you later," Freddie murmured.

Sir James ushered them into the library. "Come here Sylvia, my dear." He took Sylvia's hand and smiled at her. "This is for you," he said, putting a small box into her hand. "Go on, open it." Sylvia did so and gasped as she saw the dainty diamond watch. "It's your engagement present from Liliane and me," Sir James said. He kissed her cheek. "Welcome to the family."

Sylvia smiled, less because of the valuable gift than because of the welcome. Gail looked at her tenderly. Liliane managed a tense smile. Nobody paid any attention to the door, through which Alex Medway strode and stood looking at them with a fierce, sardonic expression.

"Well!" he exclaimed, and his voice contained a wealth of meaning.

For a blinding moment Gail saw the scene as she knew he would see it: the huge diamond on Sylvia's finger, the watch that Sir James was fastening on her wrist—these were the things Alex would notice first, and they would confirm his worst suspicions.

"This is wonderful!" Sir James cried. "We weren't expecting you back until next week."

"I got the message on my answering machine and caught the first plane," Alex said, his hard eyes going from Sylvia to Gail and back again.

He'd evidently been out in the rain. His coat was sodden, his hair plastered to his skull and in Gail's state of heightened consciousness he presented the appearance of an avenging angel.

"That's the spirit," Sir James said enthusiastically. "Come and meet your new sister-in-law."

"We've already met, briefly, at your wedding," Alex said, looking down from his considerable height to Sylvia. She seemed to flinch, as though something disagreeable in his tone had gotten through to her. "I remember you very well," he added.

Sylvia gave a little gasp and seemed to be searching for words. Gail's mouth tightened grimly. "I wonder if you remember me, too?" she asked, forcing him to look at her.

He turned, and there was something in his eyes that made her color. "Of course I do," he said. "I told you I would. Don't *you* remember?"

She recalled everything about that first meeting because it was all burned deep into her. His dark eyes, raking her, told her that the details were a living part of his consciousness, too, including the moment when she'd rejected and humiliated him. That had neither been forgotten nor forgiven.

"Get into some dry clothes before you catch cold," Sir James said. "Eh? What?" He turned as his wife laid a hand on his arm. "Oh, yes. We've had to change your room, Alex. Liliane needed somewhere bigger to store some clothes, and your room was nearest."

"After all, you're seldom here," Liliane added. "I'm sure you understand..." She fell silent under the grim, ironic look in Alex's eyes.

"I understand perfectly, mother dear," he said softly. "Did you find a suitable attic for me?"

"I'll show you," Freddie said hastily, and left the room with his brother.

There was a short silence after Alex had left. Sir James filled it with offers of more sherry, which Gail and Sylvia both refused. Sylvia thanked him again for the watch, but now her manner was awkward. The message in Alex's eyes hadn't been lost on her and she was clearly feeling uncomfortable. Gail decided to get her away quickly, before Alex made matters any worse. She rejected the thought that she might be running away for her own sake.

After awhile, Gail discovered that she'd left her purse in the dining room and hurried out to fetch it. As she crossed the hall Alex was descending the stairs, attired in dry clothes. "You seem to have walked through the storm to get here," she remarked.

"I had a punctured tire. I had to change it myself."

"In this downpour? You really were determined, weren't you?"

"Yes, and I think I arrived not a moment too soon. Do you know something? I'd have bet long odds that I would find *you* here."

"And just what do you mean by that?"

"I think you know very well what I mean. It didn't take you long to get your professional claws into my father, did it? But let me tell you this, you can forget your commission, because I'm going to prevent another disaster in this family if it's the last thing I do."

"How dare you! You know nothing about Sylvia."

"I know how her eyes lit up at the sapphire necklaces my father gave the bridesmaids. I know she hadn't been engaged to Freddie for five minutes before she was covered in jewels again. Don't tell me my father isn't picking up the bill for that ring."

"If he is, it's his decision because he's a generous man."

"Quite. And I aim to see that his generosity isn't taken advantage of."

"Can't you understand that Sylvia loves Freddie? And he loves her enough to stand up against any opposition from you?"

"We'll see." A noise from the library made him take Gail's arm and draw her back into the dining room. Still holding her, he said, "We were bound to meet again, weren't we?"

"Meaning that you think I engineered this engagement?" she replied.

"Are you daring to pretend you didn't?"

"That's right. I didn't. I tried to discourage her."

"Come, you don't expect me to believe that, do you?"

"Of course not, because it doesn't suit you. But I've warned Sylvia that Freddie's family will treat her shabbily. And I'm quite sure that you're going to prove me right."

"If, by that, you mean I'm going to protect my brother and father from another gold digger, you're perfectly correct. And I'll do it. I know Freddie better than you. I know how impressionable he is, how easily taken in. But now that I'm here, his eyes are going to be opened, do you understand that?"

Gail's eyes snapped with temper. "I understand that it's intolerable to you not to get your own way in everything. It really got your goat that Liliane dared to shift your room, didn't it? Even though this is her home, not yours."

Alex was silent for a minute, a strange light in his eye. "What 'gets my goat,'" he said at last, "is seeing Lily take over a room that used to belong to my mother. She lived in it during the last year of her life, when she was too ill to move, and I used to sit by her bed and have long talks with her. She and I understood each other, as Dad and I never will. When she died I made sure her room became mine, because there I could still feel close to her. I cherished the hope that Dad understood all that enough to keep Lily's predatory little paws off. Evidently I was wrong. Now, I think we should rejoin the others, don't you?"

Without waiting for her reply he strode away, leaving Gail staring after him, appalled.

Chapter Four

The next morning Gail was busy keeping a round of appointments. On the way back, her car phone rang. It was Jan, her secretary. "I thought I'd better warn you," she said. "There's a Mr. Alexander Medway here, demanding to see the boss. He says nobody else will do."

"Did you tell him the boss's name?"

"I didn't get the chance. I told him my employer was out and he said he'd wait. Then he took out some papers and buried himself in them as though I'd ceased to exist."

"Fine," Gail said. "Keep him there."

She hurried back, her mind seething with anticipation. Nothing more had happened the previous evening. Alex's arrival had effectively blighted the celebrations, but there had been no explosion. He'd been coolly polite to both Gail and Sylvia until they'd taken their departure, which was soon. But what had happened afterward, she wondered?

She was back at her office in ten minutes, sweeping in with her head up. Her premises were in Chichley's picturesque main street. On the outside the eighteenth-century facade had been lovingly preserved. Inside, everything was modern elegance. The reception area was decorated in pale gray, white and silver, the walls adorned with huge color photographs of wedding cakes and brides in sumptuous gowns. A low table was piled high with white, satin-covered albums, where clients could look through selections of silver, crystal and table displays.

Alex Medway sat there, incongruous amidst all this feminine finery, but apparently oblivious to it. As Jan had said, he was buried in his papers.

"Good morning, Mr. Medway," Gail said crisply. "Please come in here." She pushed open the door to her office.

"I came to see your employer," he said, following her in and closing the door.

"Oh, really? Well you should know—"

"And I'll be honest and tell you that I'm here to have you pulled off the job."

Gail drew a long breath. "Indeed!"

"I'm glad of the chance to tell you first. I wouldn't like it to come as a nasty shock."

"That's very considerate of you. But perhaps I needn't worry. My boss might decide to ignore you."

"People never ignore me, Gail. I don't allow them to. When I say I want something, then that's what I'm going to have."

"Just like you want to have your brother's wedding cancelled? How are you managing with that, by the way? I'm sure you lit into him after Sylvia and I left last night."

"You're wrong. I'm not such a fool. I let it go last night. But that engagement won't last. You can take my word for it. So for your sake it's better if you get assigned to a different wedding."

"Your consideration overwhelms me."

"Where *is* your boss? Shouldn't he be back by now?"

"Actually the boss of Nuptia Creations is a woman, and I can assure you that there's no question of my being taken off this job."

"We'll see about that."

Gail shook her head and her eyes began to dance. "For a clever man, Mr. Medway, you've been very incautious this time. Didn't it ever occur to you that *I* was the boss?"

"*You?*" His astonishment was definitely unflattering.

"Yes, me. I don't know why you assumed I was a humble employee."

"Perhaps because I can't get used to doing business with women. They always seem to me to be playing at it."

"I don't have time to play games. I have too much work on hand. I don't need your money. I make a very good living. What's more, I have my *own* gold credit card, plus a nice apartment and the ability to buy any jewels I want for myself." Her eyes glinted as she reminded him of his own words. "Does that make my position clear?"

He was pale. "You made a fool of me."

"You walked into it. You made an assumption but didn't check your facts. That's dangerous in business. You should know that."

His dark eyes gleamed with annoyance, but before he could say anything the phone rang and Gail snatched it up. "Do you want me to hold your calls while he's there?" Jan asked.

"Not at all. Please put any calls through. This conversation isn't important." That infuriated him even more, she was glad to note.

"In that case I have Mrs. Rudman on the line."

"I'll talk to her." Alex made a gesture of impatience but she silenced him with a wave. "Mrs. Rudman, I was just about to call you. I've settled everything with the caterer and..." She went on talking as if he wasn't there, refusing to hurry to please this arrogant man. Alex watched her in mounting exasperation. After ten minutes, when she showed no sign of hanging up, he took hold of the receiver. "Hey!" she said, indignant.

"How long is this going to go on? After all, I had your attention first."

"But you're not a customer. I told you I take my business very seriously, and the customer comes first." She wrenched the receiver back. "Sorry about that, Mrs. Rudman. I was just swatting a fly."

"The hell you were!" Alex growled. He strode up and down the office, glaring, until Gail concluded the conversation and hung up. "Thank you," he said with heavy irony. "Is it my turn now?"

"Not quite, yet. Just try to be patient." Gail flicked a switch on the intercom to get through to her secretary. "Jan, call the caterer about the Rudman wedding and tell him she agrees about the..."

Alex let out a long breath, but controlled his temper until Gail was off the intercom. Then he snapped the machine on again and barked to Jan, "I want no more calls put through here until I've finished."

"Hey, where do you get off giving orders to my employees?" Gail demanded.

"It seems it's what I have to do to get your attention."

"I can't imagine why you want my attention. You came here to get me fired. Now you know you can't do that, you may as well go."

He gave a mirthless laugh. "I'm not the only one who wants you fired. Lily would also like to get rid of you."

Gail stared. "Lady Medway?"

"To me she'll never be anything but Lily Hatch. She's showing her true colors, as I predicted. My poor father doesn't know his own home any more. Last night, after you and Sylvia had gone, there was a row—*not* instigated by me. Lily is furious that you've been called in."

"But why? She and I got on so well."

"That was when you were helping her get her hands on the Medway fortune. Spending it on someone else doesn't suit her at all. You saw her last night. Don't you realize I was right about her all the time?"

"I must admit, I was a little surprised—"

"Which means I won our bet."

"I don't recall any bet."

"Three months, I said."

"Well, what do you think you've won?"

The buzzer on the intercom went again. "I told you, no calls," Alex barked.

"Yes, but you don't pay my wages," Jan retorted. "Gail, Mrs. Anfield is on the line—"

"I'll talk to her," Gail said.

But before she could lift the phone Alex's hand slammed down on it. "I'll tell you what I win," he snarled. "I win an evening of your time, away from the damned telephone."

"Are you asking me out?"

"Isn't that what I just said?" He released the phone and went to the door. "Tonight. Dinner. And dancing." He rapped out the words with the staccato rattle of a machine gun. Gail listened in fascination, almost hypnotized.

"Anything else?" she asked, dazed.

"Yes," he snapped. "Wear a clinging black dress."

"I don't *have* a clinging black dress," she yelled.

"Then get one with your damned gold credit card. I'll collect you here at eight o'clock."

At precisely five minutes past eight that evening Gail sat beside Alex in his Mercedes, inwardly grumbling.

I had a real chance to put him in his place. Instead, what did I do? I went out and bought a clinging black dress at a price that will cripple me for a month. And I took an hour longer to get myself ready than I normally would. And I was at the office, waiting for him, half an hour early. I must be out of my mind.

"You look wonderful," Alex said beside her. "Just the way I've been thinking of you for months."

"I wish I could return the compliment," she said coolly.

"You mean you haven't been thinking of me?"

"I have a lot of work to do. It occupies my mind fully."

"So you think of work and nothing else, all the time? I came along just at the right moment to save you, didn't I?"

"I could certainly do with an evening out," she conceded. "Your arrival was convenient."

"Nothing more?"

"Nothing more."

"If you say so."

Their destination turned out to be a large country house set in beautiful grounds that had been turned into a night club. "Kate and Ellis Webster, friends of mine, have hired it for the evening to celebrate their thirty-fifth wedding anniversary," Alex explained.

"I know the Websters," Gail said. "I did their daughter's wedding last year."

"I might have known."

A good-looking couple in their fifties met them just inside the door, and the greetings were full of laughter and cries of recognition. "We've ordered the band to play tunes from the year we were married," Kate confided. "Waltzes and such. Our children can hardly stop laughing, but we don't care. We tell them one day they'll be nostalgic, too."

From behind them came the sound of rhythmic music. As they went inside Alex said, "Before we get something to drink, we'll have one dance first, just to remind ourselves that it's still true."

"Is it?" she said, nettled by his confidence.

But her annoyance fell away as soon as they were on the dance floor. After the first note of music she was back under the spell, swaying to the rhythm of the music, to *his* rhythm, her body curving against his as though they'd never been apart. The soft dress clung to her, outlining every tiny movement until she felt as if she were naked. She was mad to do this, she thought. She'd tamely yielded to his insistence and put herself in danger—danger of what? She didn't want to look too far ahead. But her will seemed to have slipped away, leaving only an instinct to follow his lead, an instinct that she distrusted as much as she distrusted the man himself.

When the dance was over he led her out into the garden, where the trees were hung with colored lights. There was a small patio, also decorated with colored lights, with small tables around the sides. They settled at one of these and he procured champagne and canapés.

"How did you come to be such a good dancer?" she asked.

"Through my father. When he was young, people socialized through ballroom dancing at the 'Palais de Dance.' He made Freddie and me learn so that we could meet nice girls. He didn't realize that time had marched on and dancing is done in clubs these days."

"He's a terrific dancer himself," Gail observed. "I noticed at the wedding. Liliane could hardly keep up with him."

"He met my mother at the local 'Pally.' She was entering a competition but her partner got the flu at the last minute. Dad came to the rescue, and they won a trophy for their fox-trot. They were married six weeks later."

He gave a reminiscent grin and his face softened. "I still have that trophy. They kept it on the mantelpiece. I remember seeing them about three years ago, doing the fox-trot like the night they met. They were both gray-haired and as plump as a pair of seals, but they never put a foot wrong."

"They sound as if they were really close," Gail said, hoping to keep him in this vein.

"They were. They loved each other to the end. When she died, two years ago, he was lost. Freddie and I always hoped he'd marry again, but not the way he did. We had hopes of Maud Harker. She's a family friend, a widow of nearly his own age. She'd have been suitable."

"Oh, honestly!" Gail exclaimed in exasperation. "He doesn't want someone 'suitable.' He wants what every man wants—someone who'll make him feel alive."

He lifted an eyebrow. "The way you do me?" he asked lightly.

"Leave us out of it," she said hastily. "And don't compare your situation with your father's. You still have all your choices before you. He's seizing his last chance of happiness."

"And do you think he'll be happy?"

"That's for him to say. Alex, don't do anything to spoil this for him."

He shrugged. "Like I said, the marriage is made. It'll fall apart without any help from me."

"And then you'll see the back of her, and as far as you're concerned everything will be all right. Except for him."

"Won't it be better for him to see the truth?"

"Perhaps he doesn't want to see it. He can't live his life according to your rules, any more than you could live according to his."

"Did you see how she flaunts herself as Lady Medway? Uniformed maids, calling her 'Your ladyship.' Ye gods! Dad always managed with a couple of cleaning ladies who wore jeans and called him Jimmy. And she's no happier about Freddie's marriage than I am. She had set her heart on him boosting her position by marrying a title."

"So that makes two of you who'd like to break it off?" Gail said sharply.

"Yes, but with her it's snobbery and with me it's—well, you know about that. But hell will freeze over before I join forces with Lily."

"I'm glad to hear it," Gail said distractedly. She was thinking of Mrs. Cater, who'd also been a snob, and what her snobbery had led to.

"I imagine you are," Alex said with grim humor.

After a moment his meaning got through to her, and she said angrily, "I've told you I didn't work to bring about this engagement, but you refuse to believe me, don't you?"

"It's a good match for Sylvia. As an affectionate cousin, why shouldn't you promote it?"

"Because..." She hesitated on the verge of telling him about David, but she couldn't make herself speak of it. "Because of people like you," she said at last. "Liliane too, but mostly you. I don't want Sylvia to be unhappy, which is why I've tried to warn her away from Freddie."

"From my poor little brother? What's he done that's so terrible?" Alex asked comically.

"He's too charming."

"I've often said so myself, but why should you object?"

"You've also said that he's impressionable. I'm not sure I want Sylvia married to a man who's so weak that he can be pushed around by his older brother. I'm no happier about this marriage than you are. You can believe that or not, as you like."

Before he could answer, a waiter appeared with more champagne. When he'd gone Alex said, "Perhaps we'd better get onto a safer subject while we eat."

"Perhaps we'd better."

"Tell me how *you* come to be such a good dancer," he said smoothly.

"I guess that's safe enough. Ballroom dancing is useful in my job."

"But why did you learn in the first place?"

She'd learned because Mrs. Cater had frostily informed her that David's wife should have all the social graces. She'd quickly become a skilled dancer, which had caused some difficulties since David's dancing was no more than moderate. Mrs. Cater had seized the chance to call her expertise "vulgar."

"I learned for the sake of my job," she said stiffly. "That's all there is to it."

"If that was 'all' there was to it you wouldn't have clammed up so suddenly," he said shrewdly.

"I acquired several skills because my job needed them," she hedged, "as I'm sure you did."

"I wish you could have seen your face just then," he said thoughtfully. "It shows a lot more than you realize, probably more than you want it to. You were looking at something in the distance—or deep inside yourself—and trying to make up your mind whether to confide in me. Then you decided not to, which is a pity."

He was watching her closely and she felt herself inwardly shrink from his piercing gaze. "This champagne is delicious," she said at last.

"Why are you shutting me out, Gail? Have I deserved it for being such a bear?"

"Don't be silly. The subject doesn't interest me, that's all."

"What subject?" he asked.

"I've forgotten," she said after a tense silence.

He let it drop. Behind his cool facade he was full of a confusion that matched her own. He was infuriated with himself for not being able to get her out of his head these last few months. Her stormy rejection of him had drawn a line under their relationship, *should* have drawn a line under it. Alex wasn't a man who gave any woman the chance to say no twice.

But she had refused to be dismissed from his mind. What was worse, in the last few months he had sometimes found himself minding his manners because of the way *she* would view his behavior. That annoyed him more than anything, because minding his manners was a habit he'd gotten out of. It was like being haunted by a schoolmarm, but a schoolmarm with a seductive voice and a divine body that had been created to move in harmony with his own.

When he'd heard of Freddie's engagement he'd canceled several important meetings to come hurrying back. That was to save his brother, of course. But at the back of his mind had been the thought that he was bound to meet Gail again, which would give him the opportunity to compare the real Gail to the one in his memory. With any luck the reality would prove less potent, and the memory could be dismissed.

But he'd been confounded. Their meeting at Gracely Manor the previous night had affected him so profoundly that he had actually become afraid, and tried to have her pulled off the job so that he could avoid her. Yet now, by some alchemy, here he was, sitting beside her, and she was wearing exactly the garment he'd longed to see on her. It emphasized the curves and valleys of her slim body in a way that he knew he shouldn't watch if he wanted to keep his sanity.

"Talk to me," he commanded in a strained voice. "Tell me how you've spent these last three months."

"Dreaming about you, of course," she said lightly. "Listening for the phone to ring, breaking my heart when it was never you, thinking about you night and day, wondering if you ever spared a thought for humble little me in your busy schedule—"

"All right, all right," he said, scowling. "There was no need for that."

"I thought I should get it in first, before *you* informed *me* that I was secretly yearning for you," she explained demurely. "After all, at our last meeting you were so busy telling me what I thought and felt that I couldn't get a word in edgeways."

"I ought to bear you a grudge for the way you treated me then," he observed.

"The way *I*—?"

"You could have told me that you were your own boss, and saved me making a fool of myself."

"So if you'd known I was my own boss you wouldn't have made me that interesting proposition?"

"I wouldn't have made it in quite those terms."

Her eyes sparkled with amusement. "Anyway, when a man's that determined to make a fool of himself, who am I to spoil the fun?"

"Do you think it was very kind?" he asked unexpectedly.

Gail regarded him shrewdly. "Kindness is wasted on men," she said. "And I'm too good a businesswoman to go in for waste."

"Now there's a curious statement. There's a whole history behind that remark. How fascinating it will be to uncover it."

"I doubt you ever will," she said quickly. "I didn't mean to say it."

"I know. That's what makes it even more fascinating. It's the things that slip out in an unguarded moment that contain the real truth."

"Shall we drop it?" she asked tensely.

"All right—for the moment." His eyes never left her face. "Gail, why don't we—?"

"*Gail.* How lovely to see you again!"

Alex sighed and fixed a smile on his face for Brenda, the Websters' daughter whose wedding Gail had organized the previous year. She was a strongly built young woman in her late twenties, handsome and full of energy, which an advanced pregnancy apparently did nothing to hinder.

"And Alex!" she cried. "What are you two doing together? Don't tell me. You're plotting Freddie's marriage to Sylvia. We've heard *all* about it. They *have* called you in to do it, haven't they, Gail? If they haven't, just let me know, and Jimmy and I will storm Gracely Manor."

"They have, actually," Gail said, laughing and trying to make herself heard above Brenda's enthusiasm. It was useless.

"Jimmy and I have always said it was your lovely wedding that gave us the perfect send-off," Brenda steamrollered on. "We had the most *gorgeous* honeymoon and I got preggers straight away, which we both wanted. I'll bet Sir James and Liliane are just *deliriously* happy." She clutched Alex's arm. "It's Gail who does it, you know. If she arranges your wedding, you're set for life. Everyone says so."

"Really?" Alex murmured. His eyes were glazed.

"Yes, honestly. It's a sort of spell she casts. I've got to dash. Mom and Dad will be coming out for the speeches and toasts in a minute. Isn't it lovely to see them so happy after thirty-five years?"

"You mean they've reached this state of felicity without having Gail marry them?" Alex asked with deceptive innocence. "I wonder how they managed it."

Gail kicked him under the table as Brenda hooted with laughter. Jimmy, as hefty and cheerful as his wife, arrived to carry her off for the little ceremony. When they'd gone Alex buried his head in his hands. His shoulders were shaking with laughter.

"I hadn't realized what a local celebrity you are," he said at last, lifting his head. "It seems that no wedding is complete without you."

"I'm the best in the business," Gail assured him cheerfully. "I've got the whole town sewn up."

"In what way?" he asked, genuinely interested.

"Florists, caterers, marquee owners, car hire, dressmakers, dress rental—I can get them all at a substantial discount because I guarantee them a minimum level of business every year. If the bride wants to economize on the dress she can rent one from my stock. If she wants to spend more she can choose one from the bridal department of a local store, and Nuptia Creations will buy it."

"At a discount."

"That's right."

"And if she wants to spend a lot?"

"Then she goes to Barry Fashions who designs wedding gowns, which are out of this world."

"At a price."

"Not the price he wants. I regularly beat him down. He gets a lot of business from me, and I don't allow him to forget it."

Alex gazed at her, fascinated by her crisp, efficient tone. When he tried to link this cool entrepreneur with the sensuous creature who glided across the dance floor in his arms the contrast made him giddy.

"Why are you looking at me like that?" she asked.

"I've just realized how very much I'm going to enjoy this evening," he said, getting to his feet and drawing her after him. "Much more than I'd expected."

Chapter Five

Kate and Ellis Webster came out onto the patio and their children and grandchildren gathered around them. Gail and Alex went to join the group and listen to the speeches. Their eldest son talked about his parents' marriage, how happy it had always been, and when he finished there was applause.

"Do you think my father and Lily will ever see a day like this?" Alex murmured ironically in Gail's ear.

"I doubt whether they'll be together for thirty-five years, because of his age," Gail said.

"Ten years, then? Five?"

"I don't know about Sir James and Liliane, but I do know this much. In fifty years time you and I will meet again at Freddie and Sylvia's golden wedding, and then you'll have to admit that at least you were wrong about her."

As the little ceremony ended they strolled away under the lamp-ladened trees, where colored shadows danced. "Let's call a truce," Alex suggested. "Tell me about Sylvia."

"Do I need to?" she demanded ironically. "Don't tell me you've allowed a whole two days to pass without setting detectives onto her? I thought by now you'd know where she'd been to school, how much her first job paid and when she was vaccinated against the measles. Your detectives have really fallen down on the job, haven't they?"

"I haven't employed any detectives," he said irritably.

"But you haven't given up the idea, have you? You'll probably have me investigated, too."

In the multicolored light she could make out a grin on his face, and something significant about it made her heart turn over. "No, I'm going to enjoy finding out about you myself," he said.

She tried to control her fluttering pulse and speak normally. "But Sylvia's still under the microscope?"

"Look, I know nothing at all about her. Do you blame me for being curious?"

"No, but the proper person for you to ask is Freddie."

"I've tried, but I can't get any sense out of him. Apparently Sylvia is the most wonderful, indescribable goddess who ever walked the earth. She's sweet, generous, beautiful and perfect in every possible way. Apart from that, he was uninformative."

Gail laughed at his dry tone. "Freddie's in love," she said. "He's noticed the essentials."

"So tell me about Sylvia as you know her."

"So at last you ask what she's really like—*after* forming your judgment."

"I said a truce," he reminded her, slipping an arm about her waist.

"All right. Sylvia is my cousin. She's twenty-one and has worked for me for the last two years. She's sweet-natured, honest—"

"I've had all that from Freddie," Alex said hastily. "Tell me about her family."

"She has a sister, Carol, who's married with three children—"

"Any parents?"

"Her mother's dead," Gail said carefully. She could sense the ground growing treacherous under her feet as she approached the thorny subject of Sylvia's father. But she was determined to tell this suspicious man nothing that would give him ammunition. The truth about Rex Broadbent was Sylvia's secret, to reveal to Freddie in her own time. So she simply said, "Her father lives with Carol."

"What does he do for a living?"

"He's unemployed," Gail said. "And I know you'll read the worst into that, but lots of men of his age can't get work. Besides, he's terrific with his grandchildren, and it frees Carol to have a job, which she enjoys. She says she couldn't do without him."

"All right, all right, I didn't say anything." He held up his hand defensively.

"You were thinking it."

He gave a little smile that teased her in the dim light. "You don't know what I'm thinking."

"You're thinking that I've just confirmed all your worst suspicions—" she said defiantly.

His clasp on her waist tightened and he drew her closer, under the shade of a tree. "No, that's what I ought to be thinking," he murmured. "But when I see you—and feel you—in that dress, all I can think about is you."

Gail's pulses began to race as she felt his breath on her cheek. She was as annoyed with him as ever, but it was hard to remember that when he excited her so much. Besides, he'd shown her a way to get him off the dangerous topic. So it was all right to tease him and enjoy his reactions, she told herself. She was only doing it for Sylvia. "I told you what I thought of you before—" she whispered.

"Yes, you told me, and your body told me. But they told me different things. If you didn't want me as much as I want you, you wouldn't have slapped me so hard."

"Of all the conceited—" Before she could say more his mouth was over hers, silencing her protest, demanding her compliance. Three months vanished as if they'd never been, and her blood was pounding joyfully in her veins. His ardor brought a glittering, bright edge to her consciousness, making the rest of the world seem pallid by contrast. Her successful business, her smooth-running life, all the things that made her enviable to other women, suddenly became nothing when set against the thrill of being in this man's arms. She kissed him back, not meaning to, but unable to do anything else.

He released her, but only slightly. She found herself still pressed closely against him, his mouth near to hers. When he spoke his breath fanned her lips, sending tremors through her. "You're a clever woman, Gail," he whispered. "Clever enough to keep me on edge these last few months. I've thought of you a lot. How much have you thought of me?"

"Who says I've thought of you?"

"You have. Admit it."

She raised a laughing face to him. "Perhaps," she conceded. "And perhaps not."

"Is there another man?"

"Don't tell me that would worry you?" she asked skeptically.

"It doesn't. If there *is* someone, I'll see him off. But I want to know."

"Why don't you wait and find out?" she teased. She was beginning to enjoy herself.

His eyes narrowed. "Are you mocking me?"

"Yes. But it's beginning to pall."

"Why?"

"Because you're such an easy target. It's no fun."

He stared at her. "Fun? I'm never fun."

"Not intentionally, I'm sure. But that doesn't mean I can't have fun at your expense."

"I don't allow that," he said firmly.

Gail chuckled. "What you'll allow and what I do may not be the same thing."

"Are you laughing at me now?"

"Can't you tell?" she asked, with a touch of pity.

He scowled and she laughed out loud at his bafflement. "It must be a great trial to you not having a sense of humor," she said. "It's practically inviting the world to drop banana skins in front of you."

This time he got the joke. "I hire someone to clear them away for me. Now you're not going to laugh at me any more. I have other plans."

He demonstrated by covering her mouth and drawing her close against his body. There were people close by and Gail heard a few good-natured cheers as they were spotted. Then she stopped being conscious of anyone else. Time and space dissolved in the excitement of feeling his lips move purposefully over hers, seeking and demanding, asking her questions that thrilled her. One day, perhaps, when they were alone, there would be answers to those questions, and then more questions, leading her to a wonderful place that they would share together. But for the moment she had a sudden fearful sense that they were going too quickly. Years of caution urged her to draw back, to wait and know a little more about him. Reluctantly she disentangled herself.

"Come away from here, Gail," he said huskily. "Let's find somewhere to be alone."

"No," she said desperately. "Not yet."

He laid his hand over her heart and felt its wild beating. Then he took her hand and laid it over his own heart. Gail could hear the deep, strong thud beneath his shirt. "What is it?" he murmured. "What's holding you back?"

"I can't tell you," she whispered.

"Am I such a monster?"

"No—it's not you, it's— Oh, Alex please, not now."

He sighed. "Will I find out soon?"

"Don't rush me. There are so many things—"

"So many secrets that I'm shut out from."

"You don't know me, I don't know you—"

A faint smile softened his face. "We know quite a bit. I know that I can't be in your company for ten minutes without wanting to bang my head against the wall. You know that you dislike me more than anyone you've ever known. What more do we need?"

She gave a shaky smile. "We seem to understand each other perfectly. It's just that—"

"I'm not a patient man, Gail. But," he added hastily, "I guess I'm going to have to be."

"For a while," she said.

Somewhere behind them they heard the band strike up a lively number. ''We'd better go back and dance,'' he said. ''Then at least I can hold you close, and hope for better things in the future.''

He took her hand and led her across the lawn to where there were lights, and people and safety from her own treacherous feelings. His arms went about her and their bodies joined in the dance, moving in a wordless, passionate rhythm, filled with promise for the time to come.

With four full-time assistants Gail was able to delegate a lot of her work, but she supervised Sylvia's wedding personally. Despite Sir James's insistence that no expense was to be spared, she kept a firm eye on the budget to make sure it stayed under control. She didn't want to be vulnerable to the charge of taking advantage of his generosity. In this she was aided by Liliane, who was also studying the cost like a hawk. Whenever details were being discussed Liliane always seemed to be there, suggesting that perhaps something cheaper would look just as pretty.

One day Sylvia said ecstatically, ''I told Freddie about Dad last night. He just laughed and said it didn't matter.''

''You told him everything?''

''Every single thing, I promise. He said my problems were his problems, but as long as we loved each other there *were* no problems. Isn't that wonderful?''

''Wonderful,'' Gail agreed, looking tenderly at Sylvia's shining eyes. Inwardly she was thinking practical thoughts. Now Alex had no power to spoil this wedding. Not that Alex was such an ogre these days. She was beginning to think that all might be well after all.

Sylvia had shyly ventured to suggest that she could hire her gown from Gail's stock, and had even pointed one out. But Sir James would have none of it, insisting that Sylvia must go to Barry Fashions, as Liliane had done. Gail was torn between wanting to save his pocket and a conviction that Sylvia was entitled to the best. So it was settled that Sylvia was to have a designer gown.

When it was time for the first fitting, Lady Medway insisted on driving her to Barry Fashions herself. As Gail had feared, Liliane merely wanted an early look at the dress so that she could size it up, assess its cost and criticize. "I'm not sure that that design is quite right for you," she said when Sylvia had donned the half-made garment. "Satin, you know, shows every bump and curve. Perhaps you could lose a few pounds, then it might look better."

Barry, a young man with a faunlike face and a vague manner that concealed a shrewd business brain, gave Liliane a cold glance. He'd greeted her appearance with delight, recalling how well she'd set off one of his more luxurious creations, only three months ago. But delight soon faded when she revealed a carping spirit.

"I think it looks delightful right now," Gail said. She was coldly furious at this attempt to undermine Sylvia's confidence, so reminiscent of another time, another wedding.

"Well, perhaps," Liliane mused. "You don't think it's a trifle—shall we say—overdone?"

"No," Barry snapped. "It is *not* overdone. It's perfect. Excuse me." He stepped over Lady Medway's feet with an air of exasperation that was plainly meant to be rude.

Liliane gave a little tinkling laugh. "Of course, if you say so. But when my husband was persuaded to foot the bill for this extravaganza I don't think he actually intended—oh, well—never mind."

"Nobody persuaded Sir James into anything," Gail said, keeping her temper with difficulty. "He insisted on paying for this wedding, and he also insisted on the best of everything."

"But maybe he didn't mean to be taken quite so literally," Liliane said with a chilly smile.

Sylvia was hot with embarrassment. "It *is* too expensive," she said. "I didn't think. Maybe something simpler—"

"My dear girl, it's much too late for that," Liliane said languidly. "The material is cut now. Another dress would simply increase the bill. You'll learn to fit into our family, I dare say, and then you'll know you have to think of these things. I'll wait for you two outside."

She departed amidst a cloud of costly perfume, leaving Gail ready to commit murder. Liliane had wanted to make Sylvia uncomfortable and she'd succeeded.

She and Barry rallied around to cheer up the bride and convince her that she looked wonderful. Sylvia responded politely, but a light had gone out of her eyes.

Liliane kept up the subtle attack on the drive home, chattering with apparent aimlessness, but slipping in the odd barbed remark, until Gail forcibly changed the subject. After that, Liliane let it drop, but there was a small catlike smile on her face when they bid her goodbye.

Gail kept Sylvia late at the office that evening, pouring them both a large sherry. "Ignore her," she commanded. "She's jealous."

"Jealous? Of me?"

"Of the money Sir James is spending on you, which she thinks would be better spent on her."

"It's not just that. She doesn't think I'm good enough for the family. She keeps talking about an earl's daughter she wanted Freddie to marry."

"And give her another leg up the social ladder," Gail exploded. "It's nonsense, Sylvia. I know who she means and Alex says there never was any chance of it. Freddie didn't like her. It's all in Lily's head."

"Lily? Her name's Liliane."

"Not according to Alex. He checked up and discovered that she's really Lily Hatch. I thought he was being unkind, but I'm beginning to realize he's been right about her. I've started to think of her as Lily, too."

"She's just like David's horrible mother," Sylvia ventured.

Gail stared. "Surely you never met David's mother?"

"I was there at the church. I was your bridesmaid, remember?"

"Goodness, yes, so you were," Gail said, startled. Her searing memories had focused on Mrs. Cater, blocking out the child who'd watched everything silently. "But we're not going to think that way," she said firmly. "This family is *not* like the Caters. Sir James has welcomed you as his daughter, and he's thrilled at this marriage."

"But Alex would like to see it broken off, wouldn't he?"

Gail smiled impishly. "You leave Alex to me. Under my influence he's gradually becoming human."

Sylvia brightened. "You see an awful lot of him. Do you think that you and he—?"

"No, definitely not," Gail interrupted quickly. "Neither of us is the marrying kind."

It was three weeks since Gail had gone with Alex to the Websters' anniversary party. In that time he'd returned to Chichley twice. He'd brought papers that needed the formality of his father's signature, but both times he'd swept her off for the evening. Gail found herself looking forward to these evenings more than she was prepared to admit. The conversation was always light and guarded on both sides, but the air crackled with the promise of something else, something that might be exciting if they trusted each other enough to give it full rein. Perhaps one day that might happen. Meanwhile they thrust and parried on the surface. And afterward there were the sweet, suffocating kisses that sent her home with her heart and her blood singing.

She didn't know what to call their relationship. Not love, for she was finished with love. She distrusted it too deeply to do more than make a living out of it. Besides, Alex's company brought sensations that were totally unlike those she'd known with David. In those days she'd been happy to sit sharing blissful silence with her fiancé. Occasionally David would murmur a word or two—conventional words that love had transformed to wondrous songs. It was years before she was detached enough to realize that all David's words had been conventional to the point of dullness, and wonder whether he'd really been very bright.

By contrast, Alex could fascinate her with the breadth of his knowledge and the shrewdness of his intelligence. Sometimes he spoke as one entrepreneur to another, taking her seriously as a businesswoman in a way she enjoyed.

And when she did look up to find his eyes sending her silent messages, the air was suddenly full of thrilling danger. She was adept at dispelling that danger with a laugh, although part of her was reluctant to do so. The next step would be to invite him farther along the perilous path, and she wasn't yet ready for that.

Once he'd even asked her to suggest a suitable wedding present for Freddie and Sylvia, speaking of the forthcoming marriage as an accomplished fact. Gail had breathed an inward sigh of relief, hoping that from now on all might go smoothly.

When the dress was ready for its second fitting, Barry insisted that this must take place at Gracely Manor, so that Dora, his assistant, could see his creation against "the setting of the reception." Gail offered to drive Sylvia over, and be there for moral support in case Liliane flashed her claws again. But at the last minute the car wouldn't start.

"I've just had it repaired," Gail cried in frustration. "I'll swear this wretched car is jinxed."

"Perhaps it's time you treated yourself to a new one," Sylvia suggested. "Like the one you keep looking at."

"That's just wishful thinking. It's much too expensive. I couldn't possibly justify it."

"Look on the bright side," Sylvia suggested.

"There isn't one."

"Yes, there is. With any luck, this will break down again and then you'll have an excuse."

"Very funny." Gail turned the ignition key again, and to her relief the engine started. "Life at last. Let's hope it keeps going."

Dora was waiting at Gracely Manor. She was middle-aged and efficient, and Gail had often found her motherly presence a welcome relief from Barry's vaporings. She helped her hook Sylvia into the dress. It was a beautiful, luxurious design of satin and lace that flowed into a long train. It looked perfectly in place against the magnificence of the gracious old house.

Sir James was away for a few days, and Gail had cherished the hope that Liliane might have gone with him, but to her dismay she came in during the fitting and sat with her eyes fixed steadily on Sylvia, not uttering a word. Sylvia smiled uncertainly, and Gail could see her struggling not to be affected, but Liliane's very silence was unnerving. When Dora said, "There now, isn't that lovely?" Liliane merely gave her feline smile, and a tiny shrug, as if to say that if they liked such extravagant display, who was she to comment? Gail clenched her hands, restraining an impulse to do violence on Liliane's expensively groomed person.

She was saved by the shrilling of her mobile phone. She answered it and wandered out onto the terrace to talk privately. It was Jan with an urgent query. Gail dealt with it and hung up, but instead of returning inside at once she sat breathing in the soft beauty of the summer afternoon, before returning to the scene of tension.

Suddenly she saw a speeding car appear through the trees and approach the house. She smiled as she recognized Alex's vehicle, but her smile faded as it came to a sharp halt and the man himself jumped out. He was scowling and his eyes narrowed at the sight of her. "Whatever's the matter?" she asked.

"You hoped I wouldn't find out, didn't you?" he demanded grimly.

"Find out what? Alex, whatever are you talking about?"

"I told you I had Lily investigated. You knew I'd do the same with Sylvia, so you set yourself to charm me into forgetting. And by God, you succeeded. What a fool I was!''

"Is there some point to this?" she asked, getting angry in her turn. "Are you telling me you've been spying on Sylvia?"

"*No.* I let it go, because you convinced me I was being too suspicious. But we'd both forgotten about Lily."

"Do you mean that she *dared—?*"

"She used the same detective that I used on her," Alex said grimly. "Rather neat, that, don't you think? And he made some very interesting discoveries about Sylvia's father."

"Oh heavens! Look, Alex—"

"How that man has stayed out of prison these last few years I don't know. Or rather, I *do* know. His family has rallied around to protect him, and in recent years that's meant *you.* You've paid out a fortune to keep him out of trouble, but you dug your heels in recently, didn't you? Evidently he was getting to be too much of a millstone. Was that when you decided to shunt him off onto my family?"

"How dare you!" she exclaimed hotly.

"I dare because I don't like being made a fool of. So Sylvia is honestly in love, is she? But by a charming coincidence she just happens to have fallen in love in a family that can support her father. And you! Yes, you're a good businesswoman. I have to admire the way you've turned your firm into a little gold mine."

"Since Nuptia Creations is a private firm there's no honest way you could have come by those details," she snapped.

"He's a very good detective. He gets results. He found out how often you've come to Rex Broadbent's rescue and how much it cost you."

"So *I've* been investigated, too?" she whispered.

"Does that worry you?" He noticed that she was looking suddenly pale. "What are you afraid might be discovered?"

Gail pulled herself together. "Whatever you may have discovered about me it's nothing to what I'm discovering about you. How could you do a thing like this to Sylvia—to me?"

Alex's face was dark with rage. "Very neat, but you don't get to turn the tables like that. It was Lily who set them on, not me. It *should* have been me, but I let myself be taken in by you. The subject is Rex Broadbent, a man who gives Sylvia an urgent reason for finding a rich husband, and you a motive for promoting the match. I don't blame you for wanting to get rid of the burden, but I do blame you for your methods. And I blame myself most of all for falling for your tricks."

"I've never used any tricks on you, Alex," she cried. "It was you who pursued me, but you're so eaten up with suspicion that you can only see things one way. I pity you."

"Don't pity me. Pity yourself and Sylvia when Freddie finds out the nice little surprise the two of you have been preparing for him."

"Freddie knows all about Rex. Sylvia told him everything. He said he didn't care."

Alex drew his breath in sharply. "Very clever," he breathed. "Do I detect your hand behind that neat piece of footwork?"

"If you mean did I advise Sylvia to have no secrets from Freddie, yes, I did. But she's an honest person and left to herself she'd have been bound to—"

"But she hasn't been left to herself, has she, Gail? You've been pulling the strings most of the time. We've all been your puppets, *even me.*'' Alex stopped abruptly, as though something painful were choking him. ''Well, it ends here and now,'' he said at last with a shaking voice.

''What are you going to do?'' she cried as he turned away.

He'd regained command of himself. ''Watch me and find out.''

''Alex!'' She seized his arm as he turned, but he flung her off.

''The sooner your scheming little cousin knows just where she stands, the better. I'm going to find her right now.''

''I'm here.''

Startled, they both looked up to see Sylvia standing behind Alex on the terrace. From her look it was plain that she'd heard everything. Her face was ashen against the glorious bridal white. ''I don't know what you mean,'' she whispered. ''Why are you talking like this?''

''I think you know very well what I mean,'' Alex said coldly. His eyes raked her, taking in the luxurious dress. ''And so the bandwagon proceeds,'' he said, sneering.

''Alex, stop it,'' Gail said fiercely. ''Sylvia can't take this.''

''On the contrary, I think she has a great gift for taking,'' he said, twisting her words. ''That's the whole point of marrying into this family, isn't it? To take and take. And you've done pretty well so far, haven't you? But enough is enough. I control Freddie's income. I can cut it to virtually nothing, and I will. You're not marrying a rich man. You're marrying a man with a rich father, and that's going to be no use to you when I've got through. So why don't you take what you've got and leave while the going's good?''

Sylvia had listened to this in appalled silence. Once she put out a hand as if begging him to stop, but the spirit seemed to have been knocked out of her and when she tried to speak, no sound emerged. Tears began to trickle down her cheeks.

"Save it!" Alex snapped. "It works on my father and Freddie, but not on me."

At last Sylvia found her voice. "I never schemed to get into your family." She choked on her words. "I love Freddie, but—but I won't marry him if it's going to make trouble in his family. I never wanted the jewels—or anything. I just love him. It's true." Her voice rose to a cry. "I know you don't believe me, but it's true."

"Never mind what he believes, Sylvia," Gail said. "He doesn't matter. You and Freddie love each other, and that's all that counts."

Sylvia shook her head. The action seemed to make her aware of her veil, and she pulled it off. "No, it's not all that counts," she sobbed. "I tried to believe it was—but Freddie's family matters, too. I can't make him unhappy and he would be, don't you see? Here—take this." She tore the diamond ring from her finger and tossed it to the ground at Alex's feet. He stared, and even he, Gail was fiercely glad to see, seemed taken aback.

"Take it!" Sylvia cried. "Tell Freddie I'm sorry, but I just can't..."

Sobs choked her. She whirled and fled down the steps, the gorgeous gown streaming out behind her. For Gail, time seemed to have run backward and she was watching another bride running away in anguish. The terrible vision held her frozen. She wanted to follow

Sylvia, but she could only watch as her cousin sped away from them.

Then both she and Alex saw Freddie's car appearing between the trees. As he turned the bend, Sylvia was almost on him. He saw her too late. Before he could react, she'd collided with his car. The next moment she was lying motionless on the ground.

Chapter Six

As she raced toward them, Gail saw Freddie jump from the car and throw himself down beside her, heard his terrible cry of "Sylvia— *Oh, my God!*"

Alex was ahead of Gail, running as if his life depended on it. He reached them as Freddie rose to his feet with the crumpled figure in his arms.

"Sylvia!" Gail whispered in horror. "Oh, darling, please open your eyes. Please speak to me."

But Sylvia lay frighteningly still, her face pale through the blood and dirt that stained it. Blood trickled from a wound on her head, down onto the torn white satin. Alex was staring at her, and his face was almost the same deathly color. His eyes burned like fires out of his pallor. Gail turned on him. "Now you see what you've done!" she screamed. "Are you satisfied? *Are you satisfied?*"

Freddie began to hurry toward the house with Sylvia in his arms. Liliane had appeared on the terrace and stood watching them approach, and Gail wondered how much she'd heard.

"Call an ambulance," Freddie cried hoarsely as he ran up the steps.

"Take her inside and lay her on the sofa," Liliane said. "The poor child..." But the words died on her lips at the sight of the venom in Gail's eyes.

Gail called the ambulance on her mobile phone, hurrying into the morning room as she spoke. Freddie lay Sylvia down on the long sofa and cradled her in his arms. "Are they coming?" he cried in agony.

"They said they'd be here any minute," Gail assured him, dropping to her knees beside Sylvia. Still her cousin didn't move. Freddie bent over her, kissing her face, murmuring words that Gail couldn't catch, but they must have got through to Sylvia, because at last she opened her eyes.

"Darling," Freddie said urgently. *"Darling..."*

Sylvia's lips moved in the silent word "Freddie..." but no sound emerged.

"Why did you do it?" he pleaded. "What happened to make you run into me like that?"

Again Sylvia's lips moved, and this time the listeners heard "Sorry."

Freddie tore his hair. "No need to be sorry—it was my fault—all my fault—I was going too fast—but why were you running away? For God's sake, where's that ambulance?"

Painfully Sylvia reached up a hand and touched his face. "Sorry," she said again. "Can't—marry you— should have known—forgive me..."

Freddie looked around wildly. "What does she mean? What's she talking about?" He turned back to Sylvia, but she'd closed her eyes and now lay still against his arm. "What does she mean?" he asked again.

"Perhaps you should ask your brother," Liliane said coolly. "He was talking to her just before it happened."

Freddie threw a puzzled glance at Alex. Gail followed his gaze and saw that Alex was keeping back. His appalled eyes were on Sylvia and his face was a mask.

"What's been happening?" Freddie demanded of Gail.

"It doesn't matter," Gail said urgently. "Just think of Sylvia now. She needs you. I think I hear the ambulance." This last remark was clutching at straws, but to her relief the ambulance really did appear at that moment. In the commotion of getting Sylvia onto a stretcher and carrying her out to the vehicle, the moment passed.

There was only room for one person to travel with Sylvia, so Freddie went with her, while Gail dashed to her car. But to her despair it once more refused to start. "Oh God!" she screamed, slamming her hand down on the steering wheel. At once Alex pulled open the door. "Come in my car," he said curtly.

"*You?*" She turned a look full of hatred onto him.

"You don't have to talk to me, or even notice me. Just sit there and let me take you."

Without a word Gail went and got into his passenger seat. She was shaking with shock and horror, and tears kept trying to force their way from her eyes. She fought them back, refusing to let him see her cry, but the strain was tearing her apart. When they got caught at traffic lights and saw the ambulance vanishing ahead of them, she began to thump her hand compulsively against the dashboard.

"We're nearly there," he said.

His words seemed to break the trance that held her. As the lights changed and they moved off she said, "On second thought I *will* talk to you, because I may not get another chance to tell you what I think of you. You're the most wicked man I've ever come across. To take out your spite on Sylvia—*Sylvia,* of all people—who's gentle and honest and has never hurt anyone in her life. I hate you, Alex, and if it's the last thing I do I'll make you sorry for this. If Sylvia dies it will be your fault, and I'll never let you forget that as long as you live. Do you hear me?"

"This is the hospital," he said in a flat voice. "Go and see how she is."

Gail found Freddie sitting alone in a corridor. "Is there any news?" she asked, sitting beside him.

"They've taken her away to see how bad it is," he said in a choked voice. "How could it have happened? She just came out of nowhere—I didn't have time to..." He buried his face in his hands and his shoulders shook. "Suppose she dies, Gail. And I did it."

"She won't die," Gail said, sounding more convinced than she felt. "We're a tough family."

"But she hit the car so hard—I can still feel the vibrations going through me. *What happened?*"

Gail hesitated. Although she would never forgive Alex for what he'd done she didn't want to be the one to set brother against brother. Besides, part of the blame was Liliane's. To her relief she was saved from having to answer by the sight of Liliane appearing. Alex was a few steps behind her and Gail had the feeling that he was keeping his distance. He went to stand quietly next to a wall, near enough to hear but seemingly reluctant to join them.

Liliane came to sit on Freddie's other side. "My dear boy," she cooed. "What a terrible thing to happen! We must all hope it's not too bad."

Gail guessed, contemptuously, that she was covering herself for when her part in this disaster was revealed. When Liliane tried to smile brightly at her she looked away.

"She was talking wildly," Freddie said. "She said she couldn't marry me—or did I imagine that?" He clutched his head distractedly. "No, she said it—but what did she mean about 'should have known'?"

"Freddie, don't think of that now," Gail urged.

"But I must try to understand this." Freddie looked up at Alex suddenly. "Liliane said Sylvia was talking to you just before it happened. What do you know about it?"

Alex stared at Freddie without answering. His face was ghastly. In the end it was Liliane who answered.

"I'm afraid Alex wasn't very kind to poor Sylvia. He accused her of being a scheming fortune hunter who wanted to marry into this family for the sake of what she could get. He advised her to take what she'd got so far and leave while the going was good. He said if she didn't, he'd make sure your income was cut to almost nothing."

"Don't forget your part in this," Gail said angrily. Liliane met her eyes for a moment, then turned away.

Freddie barely seemed to have heard them. His eyes were still fixed on Alex. "Is this true?" he demanded.

"Freddie," Alex pleaded in a hollow voice, "let me explain—"

"*Is it true?*"

"Yes, it's true."

For a split second Freddie stared at him in disbelief. Then his face tightened and Gail saw his hand ball into a fist. The punch he delivered was thunderous and Alex's head snapped back with the force of it. But he made no move to strike his brother back, or even to defend himself.

"You swine," Freddie breathed. "You lousy, rotten..." He swung his fist again, hard enough to send Alex back against the wall.

"Freddie, don't!" Gail cried. "Can't you see he won't fight you?"

"Let him fight me," Freddie raged. "Then I can have the satisfaction of beating him senseless."

"Do it if you want," Alex said quietly. There was blood on his face.

He staggered as Freddie struck him again, and Gail knew he wouldn't retaliate, no matter what his brother did. She hated Alex for what he'd done, and yet she thought she'd never seen so much anguish on a human face.

The click of the door made them all turn to see the doctor. Freddie walked away from Alex, who stayed where he was. He was breathing hard and his face was bruised and bleeding, but he didn't move, not even to touch his injuries.

"How is she?" Freddie demanded hoarsely.

"It's not as bad as we thought at first," the doctor said. "She has a concussion and a few cracked ribs, but mostly it's just bruising. She's going to be fine."

"Thank God!" Freddie breathed.

Gail could only close her eyes and offer a silent prayer of thanks.

"Can I see her?" Freddie demanded.

The doctor shook his head. "I'm afraid not. She can only have one person at present. I believe one of you is her cousin?"

"I am," Gail said.

"Then you can go in."

"Look," Gail said, "I know I'm her family, but Freddie's her fiancé. I'll give up my place to him—"

"I'm afraid I didn't make myself clear. It's not just because you're related to her. She's asking for you—and *only* you. She insisted on that."

"You mean she doesn't want to see me?" Freddie demanded, dazed.

"Not just at the moment," the doctor said tactfully. He turned to Gail. "Only five minutes, I'm afraid."

Sylvia was lying back against white pillows, looking drained and wretched. An ugly bruise disfigured her face, but she opened her eyes and tried to smile at Gail. "I'm fine, really," she whispered. "Sorry to be so silly."

"It's all right, darling. But do let poor Freddie come in. He's half out of his mind."

"No, I can't see him. I couldn't bear it. Try to make him understand why I can't marry him."

"He already knows what happened and he's furious with Alex."

"Oh, no—he admires Alex so much. He's always looked up to him. Don't you see that I mustn't come between them?"

Gail silenced the arguments that rose to her lips. Sylvia was in no state to talk, and besides, she'd closed her eyes. Gail kissed her forehead and crept out. Liliane and Alex had gone, but Freddie was still there, looking forlorn. "Gail—please—" he begged.

"Not now, Freddie. She couldn't cope with it. Liliane had no right to tell you the way she did. It was as much her fault as anyone's. She hired a detective and he discovered about Sylvia's father.''

''I already know about him and I don't care.'' Freddie looked at her shrewdly. ''But now I remember, *you* blamed Alex. You cried out to him, 'Now you see what you've done.' You knew it was mostly his fault.''

Gail avoided answering this directly. ''More than anything, Sylvia doesn't want to come between you. She knows how much you admire Alex.''

Freddie looked at her and she realized that the boyishness had gone out of his face forever. He was a man now, and there was something steely about him that marked him out as Alex's kin as never before. ''I've always looked up to him as my older brother,'' he said, ''but I'll never forgive him for this.''

''Do you know where he's gone now?''

''I hope he's gone to pack his bags. I told him that if he didn't move out of the house, I would. He's not my brother any more, and he never will be.''

''Oh Freddie, please, this mustn't happen. Alex thought he was protecting you.''

''I don't need his protection. I'm a grown man and I can make my own decisions.''

''He knows that now. He knows he was wrong. For pity's sake, Freddie, leave it at that.''

He stared at her. ''How can you talk like this? I thought you loved Sylvia.''

''I do love her. And I know how distressed she'll be if you and Alex become enemies because of her.''

''It won't be her fault.''

''That's not how she feels. I'm sorry, Freddie, but even if Sylvia wanted to see you, I wouldn't let you in. You'll just upset her in your present mood.''

The doctor appeared again. "There's no point in your staying," he said to both of them. "She needs to be left alone to rest, now."

Gail got to her feet. "Come on," she said to Freddie. "Let's see if we can find a taxi."

He didn't move. "I'm staying here."

"Freddie, you can't see her."

"She might change her mind, and even if she doesn't—well, I can *be* here, just in case."

Gail wished Alex was there to witness Freddie's stubborn fidelity, and understand the depth of feeling that united him to Sylvia. She put a hand on Freddie's shoulder before walking away. At the end of the corridor she turned and looked back at him sitting motionless, his eyes fixed on Sylvia's door.

Sylvia's recovery was slow. Physically she healed well, but her mind was dazed and sick. In the midst of her misery, however, she clung to her refusal to marry Freddie. Gail was amazed that her gentle, sweet-natured cousin was capable of such stubbornness.

She relented enough to allow Freddie one visit. He went, carrying the engagement ring that Liliane had retrieved from the terrace, where Sylvia had thrown it. But when he emerged after half an hour he still had the ring. He looked so wretched that Gail took him off to a nearby pub and poured a brandy into him.

"Dad's in a terrible state about it all," he told Gail, turning the ring over and over in his fingers. "When he got home and heard what had happened, he couldn't believe it at first. He's always been so proud of Alex, thought the world of him. Well, I've always known Alex was his favorite. He's inherited Dad's business genius, we all recognize that. Now..." Freddie made a helpless gesture, "It's torn Dad apart to see the truth about him."

"I wonder what the truth about him is," Gail said slowly.

"How can you ask that? You're as against him as the rest of us—aren't you?" He looked up at her quickly.

"Yes," Gail said firmly. "But he's not the only one. Don't forget Liliane's part in this. *She* set the detectives onto Sylvia. Does your father know that?"

"Yes, but she's managed to get around him. She gave him the sweet talk about how she was just concerned for the family. She claims she wasn't actually going to confront Sylvia with anything she discovered. That's the point that sticks. It was the way Alex lit into her that did the real damage. How *could* he? I've always known he was a hard man, but this..." Freddie shuddered. "Ah well, it's over now. He's gone."

Gail's heart gave a painful thud. "Gone where?"

"Back to London, I suppose. Who cares?"

"Freddie, breaking up your family like this is exactly what Sylvia doesn't want," she said urgently.

"The family's already broken up. I've told Dad I'm leaving the firm."

"*What?* Oh no, you mustn't."

"It's the only way. I realized that when I discovered what Alex had said about slashing my income. He could do it, and that's why I have to get out. I'm a good salesman. I'll get another job. And when I'm really independent of my family I'll have the right to ask Sylvia to marry me. Maybe then she'll respect me enough to say yes."

"But that's not— Oh, Freddie, this is terrible."

"It's inevitable," he said bleakly.

Gail saw Sylvia again the next afternoon. She found her cousin pale but determined not to budge. "I've never seen you like this."

"I feel like a different person," Sylvia said. "I know so many things now that I didn't know before. I should have realized it was wrong for me to get engaged to Freddie. You warned me against it."

"I don't think I exactly said that, did I?"

"You implied that I'd get the same sort of treatment that you did. Admit it. You weren't happy about my engagement, were you?"

"Not at first, but—"

"And you were right. I should have listened to you instead of..."

Sylvia ended with a little choke. Her whole body became tense and she fixed her eyes on something she could see past Gail's shoulder. Turning, Gail saw Alex standing in the doorway.

She had to suppress a gasp at the sight of him. He actually looked older. His face had a dreadful pallor and his eyes seemed sunk in their sockets. Gail had the impression that he hadn't eaten for days. He was very still, glancing from one to the other, as though awaiting permission to enter. She still hated him, Gail told herself, but the sight of him ill and hesitant, so unlike his usual bulldozing self, tore at her heart in a way that startled her.

"May I speak to you?" he asked quietly, looking at Sylvia.

"Do you really need to?" she replied, holding tightly on to Gail's hand. "It's all over."

"That's what I need to talk to you about," he said urgently, coming in and closing the door behind him. "It can't be over. You *have* to marry Freddie." Seeing

Sylvia flinch and Gail regarding him with frosty irony he backtracked. "I'm sorry," he said quickly. "Of course it's your decision but..." He took a deep breath and said with a shaking voice, "I'd better start again."

"Very wise," Gail murmured.

Alex gave her a quick look before saying to Sylvia, "I'm here to ask—no, to *beg* your forgiveness."

"It wasn't your fault," she said hastily. "I should have looked where I was going."

"I don't mean that—although if you'd died I would never have forgiven myself. I mean the way I spoke to you. It was unforgivable...." He seemed unable to go on.

"I didn't scheme to snare your brother," Sylvia said simply. "I don't want his money. All I ever wanted was him."

"I know that now."

But Sylvia shook her head. "No, you don't. You think you believe it now, because of what's happened—"

"No, I'm not just trying to put things right," he said quickly. "At least—I want to do that, too. I realize that I made a big mistake about you... about everything. When I look at the devastation about me—Freddie wretched and hating me, Dad miserable—and think that I caused it all by being pigheaded and stupid—"

"Arrogant," Gail murmured.

"What was that?"

"Arrogant," she said louder. "Not stupid, arrogant. Mind you, arrogance is a kind of stupidity—"

Alex took a deep breath, as if controlling himself. "I didn't come here to fight with you, Miss Rivers."

"That's right. We can do that afterward, Mr. Medway."

"Certainly. I'm always ready to fight with you, especially as you're partly responsible for this whole mess."

"*Me?*" she replied indignantly.

"If you hadn't misled me—"

"I did no such thing."

"You led me on," Alex said grimly. "I understand that you wanted to protect your cousin, but there were other ways of doing it."

Sylvia was looking from one to the other. "What...?" she began.

"It doesn't matter," Alex said. "It may be that I simply deluded myself into believing—that is, hoping..." He turned smoldering eyes on Gail. "You had a hidden agenda all the time. You should have been honest with me, and not let me think..."

It dawned on Gail that Alex was stumbling around, trying to say that he'd lashed out because his feelings had been hurt, but trying to hang on to his dignity at the same time. It couldn't be done, which was why he was having trouble.

"What you thought is hardly my responsibility, Alex," she said provocatively.

"I think it is. But that's not what I'm here to say." He turned his attention back to Sylvia. "I came to tell you how sorry I am, and to ask—to plead with you to marry my brother."

"I don't know," she murmured. "Can it really be all right?"

"If you don't marry him, it'll never be all right," Alex said desperately. "Freddie's leaving the firm because of this."

"Perhaps that's the best thing for Freddie," Gail observed.

"It won't be the best thing for the firm," Alex said stubbornly. "He's a damned good salesman."

"How often have you told him that?" Gail asked.

"I haven't made a practice of it," Alex admitted. "Perhaps that was another mistake. But the firm needs him, and I—I need him. I can't bear to lose my brother, and perhaps see my father turn against me because I've split the family." He turned back to Sylvia. "And whether or not I do depends on your generosity. Please Sylvia—I'm begging you."

She looked at him helplessly. "Oh, what am I to do?"

"You do love Freddie, don't you?" Alex persisted.

"Of course I love him, with all my heart but—"

"But nothing," Alex said quickly. "If you really love someone, there are no 'buts.' You can't really send him away forever, can you?"

Sylvia shook her head dumbly. Tears were sliding down her cheeks.

Then Gail heard a sound from just outside the door, and saw a shadow on the frosted glass. Quietly she opened it and glanced outside. "Quick," she said, taking Freddie's hand. "It's now or never."

In a moment she'd shepherded one brother inside and started shepherding the other out. "Hey—" Alex protested.

"You've said all you need to," she muttered, urging him out. "Now it's Freddie's turn."

"How did he get here?"

"Sssh!" she said.

Through the patterned glass they could just make out Freddie's dark checked shirt and Sylvia's pale nightgown. Somehow they seemed to have become intertwined. Words reached them, Freddie's voice saying urgently, "You're going to marry me, do you hear? That's settled...." and Sylvia's weeping.

"Oh yes, Freddie darling—yes—yes..."

"Let's go. We're not wanted here," Gail said.

Chapter Seven

Outside, Alex leaned against the wall as though he needed the support. "Are you still speaking to me?" he asked quietly.

"That's all over now," she said. "You made it right by saying you were sorry."

"So I'm forgiven?"

It seemed strange to hear Alex of all men talking in such terms, but it was still written on his face that he'd been through hell. "Say it," he persisted.

"You're forgiven," she told him. "It's all over, in the past. It didn't happen." She knew she was overdoing it, but she wanted to dispel his suffering. She'd said she'd forgiven him because he had apologized, but secretly she knew that it was his pain that had softened her heart. The sight of Alex brought low had made her long to see him restored to his old arrogant self. It was totally irrational, and she couldn't imagine what she was thinking of. But there it was.

"What do we do now?" he asked.

"We find the nearest pub." She took his hand and he followed her docilely for a few minutes, until they reached the pretty, old-fashioned hostelry in the next street. Gail bought the first drinks, a sherry for herself and a large brandy for Alex, at his request.

"I didn't even know Freddie was there," he said when they were seated opposite each other at a little table. "He must have followed me."

"It's just as well he did," Gail said. "You were doing pretty well, but it needed Freddie to clinch it."

Alex still seemed almost in a state of shock, but he roused himself enough to say, "Why is the barman looking at you so oddly?"

"Because he recently saw me trying to comfort Freddie in here," she said. "Now it's you. He's probably wondering just what sort of woman I am."

Alex gave a wan smile. "I've done a bit of wondering about that myself. You reveal a new facet every time we meet." He took a deep breath. "I owe you an apology, too," he said with an effort. "You really did try to talk Sylvia out of marrying Freddie, in the beginning, didn't you? You told me at the time, but I didn't believe you."

"Why should you? After all, everyone's lining up to marry into the Medway family, aren't they?" she asked with a touch of irony.

He winced. "All right, don't rub it in."

"Anyway, I didn't exactly try to talk her out of it."

"But you really weren't happy about the marriage?"

"Not entirely. I warned Sylvia that the family might make her life difficult."

"Because of me?"

"Partly, but not just because of you."

He waited to see if she would continue, but she seemed reluctant. He felt as if he'd been in danger of losing his life and had only escaped by the skin of his teeth. Now he was building rafts to safety. "Sylvia said something about her getting the same sort of treatment that you did?" he prompted her. "What did she mean by that?"

"I don't recall her saying it." Gail hedged.

"I do. What did she mean, Gail? What sort of treatment did you get?" She didn't answer and his brow furrowed. "Have you ever been married?"

"No," she said, a little too quickly. "To me, weddings are strictly a way to earn a good living."

"Engaged?"

She sighed. "All right. I don't know why I should tell you because it's really none of your business—"

"Don't be so prickly."

"But I was engaged once. That's true."

"And was the family like mine?"

"Some of them were."

"The unpleasant ones?" he asked wryly.

She avoided a direct answer but gave him a brief smile. "His mother was a horror, always impressing on me that I wasn't good enough for their exalted family. You'd have thought they went back to William the Conqueror, at least."

"Instead of which," Alex said, picking up her wave length, "they were self-made, like the Medways."

Gail gave a wry, reminiscent smile. "In many ways they were exactly like the Medways. Brian Cater had started from nothing and made a fortune, just like your father. His son went into the family business, like you and Freddie. David was good-looking and charming, and his mother thought he could set his marriage sights high. When he chose a humble clerk in his office she wasn't pleased."

"The humble clerk being you?"

"That's right. I tried to be good enough for him, but nothing was right for Mrs. Cater. She kept on about how I was ruining his life and I ought to be 'sensible' and give him up. But David stood by me. I thought he was wonderful for that."

She said the last words with a little wistful sigh. She was staring into the distance, and so didn't see the quick look Alex gave her.

"So what happened?" he asked when the silence had gone on for a while.

"The wedding was planned. I was like Sylvia. I'd have preferred something simple but I had a huge extravaganza foisted onto me for the sake of the Cater family dignity. And on the day..." She stopped. She was twisting her handkerchief in her fingers. It was almost impossible to speak of. Even now, sitting here with this man that her heart was beginning to cling to, the words choked her.

"On the day?" Alex prompted.

"He wasn't there," she whispered. "I went to the church but—he just wasn't there."

"You mean you found an empty church?"

"No, the church was packed with guests and family, full choir, everything. And there I was in my wedding dress, waiting to go down the aisle to my groom—only my groom had vanished. He'd made it as far as the church, but then he stood me up at the last minute, leaving his mother to tell me the news."

"Dear God!" Alex breathed. For one of the few times in his life he was honestly shocked. He waited to see if Gail would say more, but she remained silent.

Alex hailed the barman and indicated for their glasses to be refilled. When it was done he asked, "What did you do?"

"Ran away. There wasn't anything else I *could* do. I tore out of the church and kept on running and running, not even seeing where I was going. I must have run at least a mile before a policeman stopped me. He offered to take me home in his car, but at first I couldn't stop crying long enough to tell him my address. Then I found I simply couldn't remember the address. My mind had gone a terrible blank."

She fell silent again. Inwardly she was trying to calm her emotions which the events of the last few days had left in shreds. To have come so close to loving Alex, and then have to hate him, that had been hard enough to cope with. But to find herself riven with pity for his suffering just when she hated him worst, and finally to have him restored to her—all this had cast her into turmoil. She wanted to laugh and cry at the same time. It was as though someone had taken her life away, only to give it back, a bit battered, but still in working order. And now here she was, with him, her senses rioting at his nearness.

Somehow David was all mixed up in her emotions; David, who'd inspired that old feeling that she'd thought was love, and which she now knew was nothing but a girl's ignorant infatuation. Love was something else. It was what she'd just discovered she felt for this prickly, difficult man beside her, who had no charm, no smooth words to woo her, but who'd established a grasp on her heart that was so firm that it hurt. She didn't want to love Alex Medway. She wasn't even sure she liked him very much. But somehow it had happened anyway.

She was roused from her reverie by the sound of his voice. "I'm sorry?" she said.

"I said you had a lucky escape."

"I suppose I did."

"There's no suppose about it," he said firmly. "In any case you couldn't have really loved him."

"Couldn't I? Why not?"

"The man was a coward. A sensible woman can't love a man like that."

It was what she'd told herself many times, but his commanding tone annoyed her so much that she failed to listen between the words to realize that he was seeking reassurance. "But I wasn't sensible then," she argued. "When you're in love you're not sensible. All I saw was that he was like a young god, handsome and delightful and everything I wanted."

Alex scowled. It seemed to him monstrously perverse that she should eulogize her lover right at this moment, when she must surely know that his emotions were in tatters. He'd been halfway to falling in love with her—only halfway, he'd promised himself. He'd begun to think her perfect, warm, feminine, passionate and intelligent. That last was important. He knew that some men couldn't cope with intelligent women, but to Alex a woman without brains, however beautiful, was simply uninteresting. If she wasn't bright how could she possibly understand *him?*

And just when he'd made the considered decision to allow himself to fall in love, he'd discovered that she'd been holding out on him all the time: seducing him for Sylvia's sake, lulling him into a false euphoria, so that he wouldn't find out about uncle Rex. It had seemed as if the sweet, loving woman he was growing close to had been no more than an illusion, a trick to fool him. His

swift-growing feelings had been crushed back on themselves as though someone had stamped them with a
heavy boot. And it had hurt horribly.

He'd reacted with rage, lashing out at Sylvia in a way
that he was immediately ashamed of. During the
dreadful days and nights that followed, his shame had
scorched him, and the bitter encounters with Freddie
had showed him a side of himself he could hardly bear
to confront.

Worst of all, there was Gail, accusing him with scorn
in her eyes. And when he saw that, it had dawned on
him, like a thunderclap, that falling in love might not be
a matter for considered decision, after all, that it might
already be out of his control.

Now the worst had been averted and he felt as if he'd
been through a wringer. He wanted only to be with her
and hear her say that everything was all right between
them again. Instead, he seemed to have only half of her
attention. The other half was for the man who'd be-
trayed her, yet who lived in her memory as "a young
god." A desire to summon her back made him say
sharply, "What a lot of nonsense! You were a child.
You must have seen through him long ago. Don't tell me
you've been pining for him all these years."

Tell me you haven't, he pleaded silently. Tell me he's
not the reason you've stayed single for so long.

But she met sharpness with sharpness. "If I have, it's
my own business. How could you understand?"

He shrugged, covering his hurt with irony. "So you
had your heart broken. It happens to all of us."

"I'm very sure it never happened to you," she said
coolly.

"Now there you're wrong. One of the reasons I know
about gold diggers is that I've met my share."

"But you saw through them at once," she said with a little laugh. "I'm sure you were born able to spot a gold digger at a hundred paces."

"Not all of them. There was one in particular who had me fooled—I was twenty-one and I believed everything she told me. It was the greatest love of all time, we were made for each other..." He shrugged and gave a strange laugh. "The things you'll believe at twenty-one!"

"What happened?" Gail asked.

"She had someone else all the time. We got engaged. I gave her money to buy things she needed for the wedding, so she said. But the money was passed on to him. I found out by discovering them together. I overheard quite a bit. Barely an hour before, she'd been telling me how wonderful I was. Now she was telling him that I— well, let's just say she didn't speak of me in very flattering terms." He gave Gail a wry smile. "So you see, I came by my suspicious nature in a hard school."

"I guess you did," she said sympathetically. "We both did."

"Did your absent groom ever offer you any explanation?"

"I never saw him again."

"The family just left you out on a limb, without even a word?" he demanded, scandalized.

"It would have been good business practice," she said wryly.

"That's a dig at me, isn't it? Listen, I've broken contracts when it suited me, but I've always been upfront about it. Nobody ever saw *me* running for cover."

"Well, to be fair, it wasn't quite like that. His father sent me a check. That's the only way he knew of dealing with people."

Alex grimaced. "And naturally you tore the check up and hurled the pieces back at him. Very satisfying, but terrible economics."

"Of course," Gail said. "That's why I didn't do it."

His smile died. "You mean you took his money?"

"Alex, haven't you ever wondered how I got to be my own boss?"

"You mean—?"

"I'd become friendly with the woman who owned the firm that prepared my aborted wedding. I went to work for her, and later I bought her out."

He stared at her. "Using Cater money?"

"Using Cater money. Oh, I went through the stage of wanting to hurl it back at him. I actually wrote the letter—'Do you really believe that the woman who loved your son can be bought with dirty money?' That sort of thing. But then I realized that if I did that, they'd get off scot free, and I didn't see why they should. So I tore the letter up, banked the money and used it to become successful. So it looks as though you were right."

"Was I?"

"Well, you've always thought I was mercenary. Now you know just how mercenary I can be."

Alex was amazed to realize that it hadn't even occurred to him to criticize her actions. On the contrary. He felt a new respect for her business acumen. She'd done exactly what he would have done himself.

"And I'll tell you something else," Gail confessed before he could speak. "When I joined Nuptia it had no wedding-dress hire department. I founded one." Her eyes challenged him to supply the rest.

"Using the dress that—?" he asked slowly.

"Using the very same dress that I'd been jilted in. I've had it remade twice. It's still in use, one of our most popular models."

"Well, you're a cool customer, no mistake."

"That's right, I am. I wasn't always, but I am now. Cool, calculating, mercenary—"

"Cut it out. You're not mercenary, just a very good businesswoman. If I'd had your acumen I'd have doubled Dad's fortune in half the time he made it. I'm sorry for the things I said to you. I just didn't like—finding out that—things between us weren't—the way I'd thought. I realize that you were bound to protect Sylvia—"

Impulsively she reached across and touched his cheek. "Alex, it wasn't only that. Honestly. Please believe me."

He laid his hand over hers and turned his head to kiss the palm. "I'll believe whatever you tell me," he murmured. "But if it wasn't just Sylvia—"

"We still have time to find out what it is," she interrupted him quickly. "But we can't rush it."

He withdrew his hand quickly as some new customers came in, and they sat in self-conscious silence for a few minutes. Alex waved to the barman, but Gail stopped him. "Let's go," she said. "I need some air."

Outside Alex said, "Hold my hand, please, Gail."

She slipped her hand into his and realized that he was shaking. Impulsively she put her arms around him and held him close.

"When I think of what I nearly did . . ." he said, his voice shaking. "It might all have ended so badly— Dear God!"

"But it didn't," she reassured him. "It's all right now, Alex."

"But I could have been a murderer. Hold me, Gail."

She stroked his head for a moment. "Alex, dear, you've had too much to drink."

"I needed it. I was so afraid."

"I think I should take you home."

He gave a short laugh. "I haven't got one," he said. "I don't mean to sound pathetic, but since I moved out of the manor my nearest home is London."

"My home, then."

She shepherded him to her car. He sat in silence while she drove him to her little apartment in an eighteenth-century mews. She took his hand and led him into her domain, where no other man had ever been. She hadn't intended to allow Alex here, either, but he was in trouble, and she needed to comfort him.

He slumped on the sofa and drank the black coffee she made him. "Sylvia will need a new wedding dress," he said. "I'd like to pay for it, since it was my fault the old one was ruined."

"You'll get a shock when you see the bill," Gail warned him. "Sir James insisted that it must be the biggest, the best, the most— Well, you know what he's like. That's his nature, Alex. When he's set his heart on giving you something, he just rolls over you."

"I know." Alex gave a sigh. "Instead of suspecting you I should have remembered how Dad likes to overwhelm people with gifts. The thing is—"

"What?" Gail asked hesitantly. She could tell that confidences came very hard to Alex.

"He likes to make people happy, but he's got very simple ideas about how to do it. He's a lovely man, but you have to shout to make yourself heard."

"Yes, I'd rather gathered that," Gail said with a smile.

"When I was a child he used to take me to every circus that was going. He thought he was giving me treats. But I never cared for circuses."

"Didn't you tell him?"

"I didn't want to. It was just the two of us, and he took such delight in our outings together. But in the end I plucked up courage to say I'd rather go to the science museum in London."

"What did he do?"

"Immediately took me to the science museum, and tried to put a brave face on it. He was bored, but he trailed around that huge place with me for hours, asking questions and letting me explain things to him."

"What's wrong with that?" Gail asked, for Alex's manner showed that something troubled him. "You were entitled to do what you wanted, too."

"Yes, but—I've always wished that I'd managed it better. He looked so hurt, and I realized that I'd cast a shadow over his happy memories of our days together. I've always wished I'd been more careful of his feelings."

"You mustn't still blame yourself."

"But I do. He's like a big kid in some ways. You just hate yourself if you hurt him. It's odd, but for the last twenty years I've been haunted by the longing to make it up to him."

"He's going to need you in the future, when he gets to see the truth about Lily. You were right about her, Alex. She's been showing her true colors recently, although Freddie says she managed to talk her way out of it."

"Dad's still convinced that she's well-meaning, but just a bit misguided."

"It's obviously what he wants to believe. If you force him to face the truth you might take something away from him that he badly needs."

"I don't know. Maybe I should listen to you. You're a wise woman. Always assuming that I have any relationship left with him now."

"Don't exaggerate."

"I'm not. I left the house because Freddie said it was him or me, but Dad was relieved to see me go. 'Just until things calm down,' he'd said."

"And he was right. If Freddie had gone he'd have done something rash. You're the sensible one."

"Suppose I've started a rift in the family that will never heal?"

Gail saw that he was deeply hurt by the breach with his father. Would he never stop revealing new and unexpected facets, she wondered? She leaned toward him and put her hands on his shoulders. "That won't happen," she said. "This will soon be forgotten and—"

She wasn't allowed to finish. As though her touch had galvanized him, Alex drew her hard against him in a fierce, urgent embrace. Gail felt all thoughts flee as she gave herself up to his kiss. It was what she'd been wanting to do all evening and the relief of being in his arms again after their painful separation was indescribable.

"Why didn't you kiss me before?" he murmured against her lips.

"Why didn't *you?*" she gasped.

"I've been wanting to—"

"Just kiss me, Alex—"

He responded with fierce passion, raining kisses on her face and neck, murmuring incoherent words of need and delight. Gail let herself be engulfed by his embrace. She wanted him, needed him with all the urgency of deprivation. They'd so nearly lost each other for good, and now they reclaimed each other with a kind of urgent relief.

Even during Alex's most intense kisses Gail had always been aware of caution holding him back. Now that was gone and he made love to her with unrestrained desire. She responded wholeheartedly, arching against him as she felt his fingers fumbling for the fastening on her blouse, opening it and sliding inside to touch her breasts. His groan of pleasure mingled with her own gasp, then both sounds were muffled as his tongue explored her mouth deeply, flickering against the silky skin in a series of soft assaults that sent ecstasy scurrying through her. He pressed her back against the cushions, and she clasped her hands behind his head, kissing him back with urgent movements of her lips and tongue.

This was like the stream of music that connected them when they danced, except that it was much more. She could hear music now, drawing them into its thrall, making them one, as they both yearned to be. The notes were rising higher and higher, leading her on to ecstasy. In another minute she would yield to him, and to her own desires, entirely.

But he was stronger than she, or perhaps more careful for her. She felt a violent trembling go through him, and then he drew back sharply, looking down at her with hot eyes. "Gail," he said in a shaking voice, "if you want me to go, you'd better say so now."

"I don't—want you to go," she breathed. "But—but I think perhaps you'd better."

"Yes," he echoed raggedly. "It would be better. What's going to happen to us, Gail?"

She shook her head. "I don't know. Perhaps nothing."

"That can't be," he said vehemently. "We didn't find each other for no reason."

"Perhaps the reason will be revealed to us, if we're patient."

"I'm not used to being patient. But I'll wait if I have to. What are you smiling at?"

"You, on your best behavior," she said tenderly.

"It comes hard."

"I know. I think you should go home now."

"My car's still at the hospital."

"You can collect it tomorrow, when you've recovered from all that brandy. I'll take you home."

She drove him halfway up the drive of Gracely Manor, to within sight of the house, but wouldn't come any farther. "Good night," she said.

He leaned over and kissed her. "Thank you for more than I can say. I'll call you."

Lights came on as he began to walk to the house. Evidently someone had heard their arrival. She stayed a while to see what happened, and saw doors open. Sir James appeared and stood waiting in tense stillness, Freddie beside him. Then Sir James enveloped his older son in a bear hug, and Freddie clapped him on the shoulder. Gail smiled to herself and drove away.

Chapter Eight

After Alex's return to Gracely Manor, he was a reformed character, which, as Gail told him, filled her with suspicion. He only laughed, and she rejoiced in the sound.

He grew secretive about his wedding gift, telling nobody until the papers were ready to be signed. Sir James was now assigning some of his remaining stock in Medway Industries to Freddie. Gail wondered how Alex felt about this until she discovered that Alex was adding to it, handing over part of his own share as his wedding present. Freddie's independence was now secure. Or, as Alex put it, "The firm will keep the best salesman it ever had."

But for Gail the sweetest moment came with the discovery that Alex's shares had been transferred to Freddie and Sylvia jointly. Not even Sir James had thought of that.

He put himself out to be nice to Sylvia, and joined in the preparations for the wedding, with never an ironic word or look. Liliane was making herself scarce these days, and her trips to London had grown more frequent. Sir James explained his wife's absences with bright, trusting comments, and to Gail's relief Alex said nothing to disillusion him.

Alex was on his best behavior with Gail, too, taking her out for the evening and dazzling her with lively talk. She hadn't known he could be so entertaining, or tell a funny story so well, and at first it was a delight. But gradually she realized that it was a way of keeping a safe distance between them. They were both waiting for whatever might happen to them next, both determined not to rush it or be overcome too soon by passion. Sometimes she would see him watching her intently over his wineglass, his eyes full of promise and question. But before she could take him up on either, the look would vanish, and she would know that the time hadn't come, yet.

He spent most of his time at the London office, but sometimes he would arrive in Chichley without warning in the middle of the day. That was how he came to drive into the parking lot behind Gail's office one morning, to find her standing there looking distractedly at a pair of legs in overalls that were protruding from beneath her car.

"What's up?" he called, halting beside her.

"My car's broken down yet *again,*" Gail said frantically. "I've got to be there in ten minutes."

"This ain't gonna be ready in ten minutes," informed the muffled voice from under the car.

"Oh, Lord! I don't need this. I really don't."

"Calm down," Alex advised. "Get into my car. I'll take you."

"Thank you," Gail said with sincere gratitude as she got in. "Everything's going wrong today."

"Where are we going?"

"Barry Fashions. It's in Monlow Street. It's the new wedding dress. Sylvia's lost so much weight since Barry measured her that it's got to be smaller. Since she's not well enough for a fitting, I said I'd do it. We're the same height and coloring, and now that she's thinner we're the same size, too."

After a few more minutes she said, "There, on the left. Thanks, Alex. It was nice of you to come out of your way for me. I won't hold you up any longer. I'll get a taxi back."

"Hey, am I being given the brush-off?"

"Of course not. But I know how busy you always are—"

"Gail, what do you think I was doing at your office?"

"I hadn't thought. I've been so frantic."

"Well, think now. I came to suggest that you have lunch with me. So why don't I come in and wait, and we'll find a restaurant afterward?"

"All right. If you're sure you don't mind waiting."

As they stepped into the hushed interior of Barry Fashions Alex asked, "Why couldn't he have brought the dress to the house for Sylvia to try on, like he did before?"

"That's what I asked him, but I couldn't get a straight answer. Apparently he's got some new device installed which means the dress has to be fitted here and nowhere else. He was very mysterious about it."

"And you let him get away with that? Surely you're the one in charge?"

"Nobody's in charge of Barry. He goes his own way." She chuckled. "And if you want the truth, I'm curious."

A young man with a delicate face burst out on them from an inner room and embraced Gail. She introduced him as Barry. The two men shook hands and Alex had a feeling that he'd been professionally sized up. Some nervous instinct made him say quickly, "I'm not the groom."

Gail burst into laughter. "You said that like a horse shying at a fence. He's the groom's brother, Barry, and he brought me here because my car broke down."

"I was devastated to hear about poor Sylvia," Barry said. "You're sure she's going to be all right?"

"She'll be fine in a few days," Gail assured him.

"And she's exactly your size?"

"Exactly. Just imagine I'm her. What's this new device you've got? I'm dying of curiosity."

"All in good time, darling. Let's put the dress on you first."

Gail vanished with Barry through mirrored double doors, and Alex took a seat, trying not to feel uncomfortable in the thickly carpeted surroundings. A long wall of mirrors faced him, and after a while he moved, seeking a place where he couldn't see his own reflection. When he'd moved several more times he realized it wasn't possible, and buried his head in a newspaper, trying to ignore himself.

After what seemed like an age Barry reappeared, calling over his shoulder, "All right, come in and let's see how it moves."

Alex glanced up idly. The next moment he'd stiffened, in a state of total shock.

A vision had appeared in the doorway. The dress was long and full in the skirt, made of white satin, covered with flowers embroidered in glittering silver thread. It was superficially demure, being high in the neck and long in the sleeves. But it was also shaped close to the body, revealing the tiny waist and high, firm breasts. A lace veil framed her face and streamed down her back almost to the floor

Alex held his breath, realizing with a sense of wonder that what he saw was Gail and, yet, not Gail. This was a creature of ethereal beauty and lush physical promise, both together.

"Now move, darling," Barry commanded. "Head up. Straight back."

Gail walked slowly forward with a rustle of petticoats, and her gorgeous reflection glided with her down the length of mirrors. At Barry's command she turned and the dress and veil swirled out, enveloping her in a cloud of foamy white. Alex felt as though something was constricting his breathing.

Barry adjusted a miniscule detail, before saying, "Right, now for the revelation of my big secret. We go through here. You too, if you please, sir."

"Me?" Alex was startled.

"I need your help, just for a moment."

Barry threw open another set of double doors and led them into a long dark room, where there were no windows. When the doors were closed everything was completely dark. "Are you ready?" he called. "Then voilà." There was a click and the lights came on.

Gail gasped as she looked around her. The room had been done up to resemble the inside of a church. At the far end was an altar rail, stained glass windows had been set a few inches from the walls, with lights behind them, and an "aisle" with black-and-white tiles swept down the center. Barry watched their astonishment with the glee of a child. "A wedding dress is designed to be seen sweeping down an aisle, so I had an aisle installed," he explained. "Now sir, if you wouldn't mind giving us your help—"

"What do I have to do?" Alex asked.

"Just go and stand by the altar rail and be the groom. I like to get the ambience right."

"No, Barry," Gail said in a suddenly tense voice. "There's no need for this. The dress is fine."

"The dress isn't fine until I say so, darling," Barry said sharply. "You've got to look like a real bride going down the aisle to a real groom."

"I don't see why," Gail insisted. Her mind was whirling. She'd steeled herself to cope with today, for Sylvia's sake. As she'd slipped the dress on she'd defied the memories of the last time she'd worn a wedding dress, and she'd got the better of them. But she couldn't cope with this, not the atmosphere of a church, and a groom waiting. "It isn't necessary," she said stubbornly.

"What a fuss you make about nothing," Barry complained. "It won't hurt you to humor me, will it?"

"It's bad luck," Gail said desperately. "I don't want to do it. The dress is fine, and it's time I got out of it and back to work."

Alex laid a hand on her arm and discovered that she was trembling. "Does it still upset you so much to think of him?" he asked softly.

"It's not him, it's—everything," she said jerkily. "Oh, I'm being silly. All right, Barry. Let's get on with it." In a flash she was her usual brisk self again. Alex watched her, a frown in his eyes.

Barry called George from his workroom and told the elderly man to escort Gail down the aisle. Dazed, Alex went to the altar rail and stood there. Barry produced a bouquet of white flowers, which he handed to Gail, and switched on a cassette player. The sound of an organ playing "The Wedding March" filled the room. "Wait for it!" Barry yelled, hurrying to get himself into the best position for viewing the dress. "Right. Gail, there's your groom at the altar, full of ardor and impatience. Now, keep your eyes on him, and step off on the left foot. Begin."

Gail tried to blot out what he was saying, and concentrate on doing her job. This was the last thing in the world she'd wanted to happen, but she wasn't going to give in and make a fool of herself. She drew a deep breath, took George's arm, and stepped forward down the aisle.

"Look at your groom's face," Barry called. "That's what every bride does. She wants to see his eyes full of adoration at how gorgeous she looks."

Feeling self-conscious, Gail raised her eyes to Alex's face, and something went through her at what she found there. He was staring as if he'd never seen her before. His lips were slightly parted, like a man who was poleaxed and needed to breathe. No bride could complain of a groom who watched her advance with that look, she thought. If only...

If only David had waited for her like this? *No.* Gail realized that David's image was gone. The groom waiting for her was Alex, and it was Alex whom she wanted. Alex and no one else. If only this were real. If only she could be sure of what his eyes were telling her. Was he merely surprised, or was he, too, thinking that this might be their own wedding?

Barry was hopping about like a cricket, now taking the dress's train like a bridesmaid, then dropping it and bouncing in front of her to watch the dress approach. Finally he assumed a clerical mien and became the clergyman.

"When the bride reaches you," he said to Alex, "you both turn and face me, standing side by side. That's right." He raised his voice to address an unseen congregation, "Dearly beloved, we are gathered here to join together this man and this woman in holy matrimony..."

To join together this man and this woman. The words echoed in Gail's head. How many weddings had she attended professionally? How many times had she heard those words? Now they rang with a new significance. She'd shunned all thought of marriage. Weddings were strictly a way of earning her living. But the thought of Alex and herself, joined in love for all eternity, suddenly took her breath away. If she were the marrying kind—which she definitely wasn't—then the man standing beside her would be her choice, the man her heart wanted and her body longed for.

If their relationship had been different she might have dared allow some of this to show in her eyes, but with Alex it was too risky. They still had a long way to go before they could find each other, and perhaps they never would. But for the moment she let herself be caught up in the unexpected beauty of the moment. If only—

"Are the sleeves too tight?" Barry demanded. "I need to see you bend your arm to receive the ring. Do you have the ring?" he asked the groom.

"I don't carry one with me." Alex was startled into answering.

"Here." Barry produced one from his pocket. "Take the bride's left hand and put the wedding ring on her finger." He ducked so that he could look closely at the sleeve. "Go on. Do it now."

Gravely Alex took Gail's left hand and slipped the ring onto it. But for some reason he didn't release her straight away. Instead he stood looking down at their clasped hands, as if frozen in time. Gail's heart began to beat hard. If only she could see Alex's face, but his head was bent. There was only the trembling of his hand to tell her that he too had been overtaken by some strong emotion.

At last Barry stood before them again and said, "All right. That's it." His eyes gleamed with sudden mischief. "You can kiss the bride now."

Gail gave a little gasp of dismay, knowing how this would seem to Alex. He wasn't the man to bear practical jokes with patience. But before she could think of a way out of this Alex said quietly, "Thank you," and drew her toward him.

He kissed her tentatively, his hands on either side of her face, being careful not to crush the lovely veil. Gail felt his lips brush hers so lightly that the kiss was gone before she was fully aware of it. She looked up into his eyes and saw a flame burning far in them. An uncontrollable sigh of longing broke from her, and the next moment his lips touched hers again.

They'd shared many kisses, but never one like this. His manner was almost reverent, as though the sight of her bridal beauty had put him in awe of her. A man invited to pay homage to a goddess might have kissed the hem of the deity's garment as Alex kissed her now. He released her mouth and she looked again into his eyes. What she saw there now was uncertainty, almost humility. And something else—perhaps a kind of worship.

Hardly knowing what she did, Gail laid her hands on his arms, and felt him shaking like a leaf through his clothes. She swayed toward him, silently pleading for it to last forever. Whatever else life might hold for her she wanted this to live with her always, the moment when Alex had looked at her as though he'd never seen anything so wonderful, and kissed her like a bridegroom, trembling with the violence of his emotion.

Alex felt as if he was moving in a kind of trance. It had started when Gail appeared in the wedding dress, herself and yet not herself, transformed into a vision. He'd understood her reluctance to go through with this, with its memories of that other wedding that had so nearly happened. It had disturbed him to think that the past still had such power over her, and for the thousandth time he'd wondered what David Cater could have been like.

When he'd seen her gliding in a cloud of frothy white beauty he'd known a surge of anger at the man who could have had this and had thrown it away. Then everything else was forgotten in the wonder of it. This was how she would look on the day she married, and it had gone through him like a bolt of lightning that the man who saw her coming down the aisle must be nobody but himself.

When Barry had told him to be her groom he'd been almost afraid, as he would be when she was really his bride. The music, the surroundings, the veiled beauty of the woman beside him had blurred his sense of reality, and for a moment he really stood in church, promising to love and honor her forever, and listening to her bind her life to his. The force of his feelings made his head swim, and when he kissed her his whole heart was in it.

"Gail," he whispered. The words "My wife," sprang to his lips and he forced them back. This wasn't the moment. That was still to come.

"All right, all right, don't make a meal of it!" Barry said with a loud laugh.

Alex cursed inwardly as his dream was smashed by the coarse comment. For a moment he wanted to sock Barry on the jaw. Then he controlled himself and forced a smile, releasing Gail.

Gail returned to earth with a sense of shock. She'd been floating in some beautiful place where there was only herself and Alex, pledging themselves to each other forever. The abrupt ending was painful, and she had to blink back the tears, praying that Alex wouldn't see them. What would he think?

"Have you found out everything you want, Barry?" she asked in a strained voice.

"Yes, it's all fine. Just a couple of minor adjustments. Call me and we'll arrange delivery."

"Then I'll get changed at once," she said and turned away, not looking at Alex. She was afraid of what she'd given away.

Alex left Barry abruptly, without a word. He was still furious at the designer for his clumsiness. He wandered out into the waiting room and drummed his fingers.

The next moment he tensed suddenly as he heard Gail's voice from behind a curtain. "You shouldn't have done that, Barry."

"Done what?"

"Telling him he could kiss me."

"Oh, you wouldn't deny me my little joke, would you? Besides, he was dying to kiss you. I was just putting him out of his misery."

"That's nonsense," Gail exclaimed with a vehemence that startled the listening Alex.

"Didn't you want to kiss him, too?"

This time Gail sounded almost angry. "And that's even worse nonsense."

"Why? Don't tell me you've never kissed him before? *Surely*—"

"That's none of your concern. You shouldn't play with people's lives, Barry."

"All right, let's just say it was business," Barry said. "I couldn't pass up the chance to sell another wedding dress."

"There'll be no wedding dress for me," Gail said quickly. "Not ever."

"Oh, come on—"

"Not ever," Gail repeated emphatically.

"Always the wedding arranger, never the bride," Barry trilled. "I'm intrigued."

"The dress is fine, Barry," Gail said. "I'll tell Sylvia you've outdone yourself."

"Spoilsport."

Alex stood very still. Something in Gail's voice, a touch of emphasis that was just a little too strong, had made all his senses alert. He listened, motionless, to hear if she would say more, but there was no sound, and after a moment he moved away and went to wait for her in the car.

He remained deep in thought for the rest of the day. Part of him had withdrawn from her. He was horribly conscious of how much he must have given away during the wedding scene. He'd even come to the verge of calling her "My wife," and surely she must have felt that in his kiss. He was glad now that he'd avoided the words. She hadn't merely been upset because of her memories. She'd actually been angry with Barry for forcing her into that position. If she was so set against marriage...

The uneasy thoughts churned around and around inside him as they had lunch. Several times she had to rouse him. He smiled brightly and forced himself to talk normally, or at least as normally as he could manage, but soon his mind would slip again, and he would sink back into a trance, never noticing the looks Gail gave him, which were at first puzzled, and then hurt.

In a few days Sylvia was home from the hospital. Gail's first job was to arrange for Barry to send over the wedding gown. "There!" she said proudly, displaying it for Sylvia. "Isn't it beautiful?"

"It's magnificent," Sylvia said softly. She stood looking at the dress on its hanger.

"Try it on," Gail urged.

She helped Sylvia into the dress and stood back to admire her. "You look wonderful," she breathed. "Overwhelming."

Sylvia began to get undressed. "I'd like you to put it on," she said.

"Me? But it's yours."

"But I can stand back and see it better on you."

Gail assented, but only reluctantly. She didn't want to wear this dress with the treacherous thoughts it could evoke. It had induced a kind of madness in herself and Alex, a madness that was best forgotten. But she couldn't explain this to Sylvia, so she put everything on, including the veil, and paraded up and down while Sylvia studied her.

"You're right," Sylvia said at last. "It is overwhelming."

Afterward Gail couldn't understand why she'd failed to heed the warning. Perhaps it was because she was so unused to her gentle cousin asserting herself. At any rate it came as a total surprise when, the next day, Sylvia came into the office.

"You shouldn't be here," Gail said. "You're not well enough to work, yet."

"I haven't come to work," Sylvia said. "I want to show you something."

She vanished into the room where the gowns for hire were kept. It was ten minutes before she emerged, wearing a long, white dress. "What's that?" Gail asked, bewildered.

"It's my wedding dress," Sylvia said.

"But—we've got your wedding dress."

"No, it's *your* wedding dress. I mean, it's the one you chose and Sir James urged on us. It's gorgeous and magnificent, but it's not me."

"Has Liliane—?"

"It's got nothing to do with Liliane," Sylvia said quickly. "I just prefer this dress. I've always had my eye on this, really."

"But it's an ordinary hired dress," Gail protested on the verge of a wail.

"I can't help that," Sylvia said firmly. "It's *me*."

The garment was cut on simple, classic lines. It was shaped into a high waist, from which it fell, without decoration, to the floor. The material was good but unadorned. Reluctantly Gail realized that her cousin was right. This simple garment really did express something about Sylvia's essential truth.

"I can't understand how I came to get it so wrong," she said helplessly.

Sylvia smiled. "I can. The dress you chose isn't my wedding dress. It's yours."

"Whatever are you suggesting?" Gail demanded, aghast.

"Darling, don't look like that. I'm not saying you consciously chose it for yourself. It's just that— well—" she faltered a little under the glint in Gail's eye "—it's completely in your style, glorious and regal."

"Hmm!"

"Well, it's true," Sylvia said with a little rush of defiance. "Weddings are in the air, and it makes people think—of wedding dresses," she concluded lamely.

"You can take that matchmaking look off your face," Gail said firmly. "I am *not* planning a wedding for myself."

"No, dear. But if you did, you've got the perfect dress for it." Reading wrath in Gail's eye Sylvia hastened to change the subject. "I'll just get changed and book this dress out to me," she said, sounding businesslike.

There was no doubt that Sylvia had altered in the last few weeks, Gail thought when she was alone. From somewhere, she'd gained confidence, and it made her speak thoughts that Gail was refusing even to think.

She couldn't tell Sylvia of the change that had come over her relationship with Alex since the day she'd worn the wedding gown. He'd been distant during their lunch afterward, and it was obvious that he was embarrassed by what he took as a trick to trap him into marriage. In the week since then she hadn't seen him. But that was good, she told herself. Now she knew where she stood, and when they met at the wedding they would do so simply as friends.

To calm herself she switched her mind to business mode. Naturally, she would have to buy 'her' dress from Alex, who was paying for it. After that it should be put into stock and hired out. At least then it would be put to some practical use. Yes, she decided. She would do that.

But not just yet.

Chapter Nine

Alex called his personal assistant into the office. Sheila was in her mid-forties, had worked for Medway Industries for twenty years and knew more about the firm than anyone except Alex himself. "Does the name David Cater ring any bells with you?" he demanded.

She wrinkled her forehead. "There was Cater and Son, that we had a bit of a battle with recently."

"Yes, I remember. But what I can't remember is whether there was anyone called David."

"I'll find out."

She was back within a few minutes, with a file. "David is the son," she said. "He was bidding against you to take over Dickson Haulage about two months ago. In the end you said to let it go because there were other haulage firms, and this one was overpriced."

"That's right. Find out how things stand concerning that affair, please."

When she returned she said, "Dickson's made a deal with Cater and Son which is all but complete."

"What does 'all but' mean?"

"The final papers haven't been signed. Dickson's wanted to be paid cash. They're only selling out because of financial problems. But Cater is only offering part cash and part shares. Dickson's held out to the last minute in the hope of a better offer, but Cater's dug their heels in."

Alex's eyes gleamed. "Get me Joe Dickson on the phone, fast."

Two minutes later he'd laid out his plan and was listening to gasps from the other end of the phone.

"Look, I couldn't do that," Joe said. "Not at this stage."

"Cash, Joe," Alex said. "A banker's draft in your hands this very afternoon. Much less troublesome than shares."

Joe gulped. "That's rough dealing—I mean, letting Cater's down at the very last minute."

"Don't worry," Alex said smoothly. "Letting people down at the last minute is something they understand."

"I'm not with you."

"It doesn't matter. Look Joe, I'll increase the price by ten thousand and you can have the draft at once. Can you really afford to turn me down?"

"Not really, Mr. Medway. And I won't deny that I'm tempted. It's just that—well, there's this big 'do' tonight, at the Caters' house. They've just moved into a new place, and it's a housewarming really, but we're signing the papers, as well. Then everyone slaps David Cater on the back and tells him how clever he's been."

"Isn't he usually clever?" Alex asked.

"Well, between you and me, he's not the brightest lad in the world. It's not often he pulls something off without help, so they like to make the most of it."

"Better and better," Alex said.

"Yes, but I'm not a brave man, Mr. Medway."

"You don't have to be, Joe. Just leave it all to me. Be at my office with your lawyer at four o'clock. Goodbye." He hung up before Joe could reply.

When he explained his plan to Sheila she regarded him severely. "How are you going to get that amount of cash available in three hours?"

"Borrow from the bank, using the Parkinson shares as security."

"The most profitable shares you own?" she gasped, outraged.

"That's why they're good security."

"But you'll be paying a fortune in interest—Dickson's isn't worth it."

Alex's eyes were alight. "It is to me," he said.

"I wish you'd tell me where we're going," Gail said.

"You'll find out when we get there," Alex teased, his eyes fixed on the road ahead. Actually he was intensely conscious of her sitting in the car beside him, looking gorgeous in the black gown he'd made her buy, her hair piled high on her head except for a few curling tendrils that whispered sexily against her neck. The subtle perfume that wafted from her heightened his enjoyment. He was looking forward to the evening ahead.

"I must be mad," she said, half grumbling. "You call me just as I'm going home, order me about like a sergeant major—"

"I simply invited you out for the evening," he protested mildly.

Gail laughed. "You didn't invite me out. You *informed* me that we were going out, commanded me to dress up and said you'd collect me at eight. I wasn't given any say in the matter."

"Well, you don't object, do you?"

"Would it make any difference if I did?"

"Not the slightest," he admitted with a grin. "You look fabulous, by the way. Just the way I wanted."

"What are you plotting, Alex?"

"How suspicious you are, just because I paid you a compliment!"

"You don't pay random compliments. You're up to something."

Alex just laughed.

At last they reached their destination—a mansion set back from the road, approached by a curved drive. Lights were on all over the house, and cars stood in the driveway, showing that many of the guests had already arrived. Just ahead of them a luxuriously dressed woman was getting out of a Rolls-Royce. The smell of money hung like a miasma over everything.

"Before we go in," Alex said, "I've brought a gift for you."

Gail stared as he opened a flat box, revealing a heavy gold necklace, studded with diamonds and rubies, lying on black velvet. Matching earrings and a bracelet completed the set.

"Alex!" she gasped. "They must have cost a fortune!" Then she clapped a hand to her mouth as Alex laughed out loud. "I didn't mean that—at least— knowing how you feel about—"

"And to think you once accused *me* of thinking of nothing but money," he said wryly.

"You know I didn't mean that. It's just that it's so unlike you to—to—"

"To give expensive presents," he interjected with a grin. "That's right, turn the knife."

"Well, you don't believe in it, on principle, in case you're dealing with a gold digger," she said, gathering her fractured dignity around her.

"But as you once pointed out to me, you can afford to buy your own jewels, so I know you're not a gold digger."

"Is that the only reason you know it?" she asked wistfully.

He kissed her lightly. "You know it isn't. Everything's different now. I've come to know you better."

Her heart soared with happiness to think he'd learned to trust her at last. "Put them on for me," she begged.

He did so, taking the opportunity to brush his fingers against her bare neck, and enjoying the shiver of pleasure that ran through her. Impulsively he dropped a kiss on the nape. His adrenaline was flowing at the thought of the evening ahead. He didn't know when he'd felt more exhilarated.

When he'd parked the car he drew her hand through his arm and they climbed the broad stone steps together. A man stood in the wide doorway, collecting invitations. Alex grinned at him. "I'm here on behalf of Joe Dickson," he said. "He couldn't make it, so he sent me instead."

The man looked uncertain but passed them through. "Who's Joe Dickson?" Gail asked.

"Never mind. Everything will be made plain. I think you might enjoy this evening."

His mysterious manner puzzled Gail and made her feel slightly nervous. Then she scolded herself for being too suspicious. If Alex had learned to trust her, it was time she also learned to trust him.

Then she saw David Cater.

In the same moment he saw her and his jaw dropped. He'd aged more than the nine years since their parting. His waistline had advanced and his hairline retreated, and a vague air of foolishness hung over him. Gail wondered if his jaw had always been so slack or whether that too was a recent development. Where was the young god she'd loved at eighteen? Vanished forever, to be replaced by this prematurely middle-aged man who looked as though life baffled him.

Her lips moved in the silent word "David." At the same time she became aware of Alex watching her closely. Until then it might have been an accident, but in a blinding flash of understanding, Gail *knew*. She whirled to confront Alex. "What have you done?" she demanded in a low voice.

"Nothing, yet," he said. "Wait for the fun to start."

"*Fun?* You *are* plotting something. Alex, I want to know what's going on."

"Excuse me," said a voice from behind Gail. "I understand that you're here on behalf of Mr. Dickson." Gail turned to face the speaker and saw Mr. Cater, David's father. He didn't react to the sight of her. Perhaps he didn't recognize her.

"That's right," Alex said. "Joe couldn't make it tonight, so he sent me on his behalf."

"Yes, but you do understand why we—er—?"

"Don't worry," Alex assured him smoothly. "I'm fully empowered to act in the matter of Dickson's Haulage. Have you met Miss Rivers?"

Mr. Cater gave a small start at the sight of Gail, who finally impinged on his consciousness. "Why, yes," he said uneasily. "I believe—"

"It's been some years, Mr. Cater," Gail said calmly. She had herself in hand now.

"You're looking very well," he said politely.

"*Very* well." Mrs. Cater had appeared at Gail's elbow, and she had plainly recognized her at once. Her eyes were cold and cynical as she looked her up and down, taking in the expensive dress, the gold jewelry. The two women met each other's eyes, the old hostility undiminished. "You seem to have prospered, Miss Rivers. I'm sure you worked extremely hard to achieve your position—whatever it is."

The words were plainly meant to be insulting, but Gail wasn't the shy girl of their last encounter. She faced her old enemy with her head up, and a slight smile hovering on her lips. "I can remember when you too worked very hard to achieve your aim, Mrs. Cater. I do hope you feel the result was worth it."

From the ugly, mottled flush that swept Mrs. Cater's face Gail guessed she'd touched a nerve. But the older woman said harshly, "I removed an obstacle to my son's future. It was well worth it."

"I don't believe I have the pleasure of knowing your son," Alex said smoothly. "Perhaps you'd introduce me to him."

"David!" Mrs. Cater's tone was practically a command. Her son came forward, smiling fixedly. A young woman with a shrewish expression pattered after him, sticking close. "This is Mr.—I don't believe I heard your name?"

"I didn't give it," Alex said. "It's Medway. Alex Medway."

At the name Medway a frisson of unease went through David and his father. Gail noticed but didn't understand it. Before either of them could say anything Alex had shaken David's hand, and exclaimed heartily, "You must be feeling quite a sense of victory tonight. Tough dealings. Joe told me he held out for better terms but you held firm."

"I offered what I felt the firm was worth," David said. "But Mr. Medway, are you—?"

"What it's worth and not a penny more," Alex said. "That's the only way to do it. I admire a man who can stand firm."

Mrs. Cater smiled complacently. "My son is known for his firm dealings," she declared.

David looked as if he wanted the floor to swallow him up, but his mutter of "Mother, please—" was drowned out by a guffaw of laughter from behind them.

A red-faced man turned sharply, colliding with Mrs. Cater. "Sorry Mrs. C," he said jovially. "A touch too much of the old vino."

"So I perceive," she replied acidly.

The shrewish young woman at David's elbow was nudging him. "May I introduce my wife, Jeannette?" he said hastily.

Jeannette greeted Gail in a nasal whine. "Any friend of my hubby's is a friend of mine," she intoned.

David grimaced, and muttered out of the side of his mouth, "I've told you before, don't call me your hubby."

"Oh, don't be such a spoilsport," she chided him. "Go and fetch me a nice little drinkie."

"Don't you think you've had enough?"

"'Course not. It's a celebration."

The red-faced man said loudly, "Don't forget the rest of the family, hey-hey-hey!" His guffaws echoed around the room, making heads turn. Mrs. Cater closed her eyes.

Jeannette giggled inanely. "This is my brother Lionel, and this is my brother Jeffrey, and those are my brothers George and Brian."

The brothers were simply versions of each other—fatter, thinner, taller, shorter—they were all red-faced and loudly jovial. Whenever one of them opened his mouth Mrs. Cater winced. When they called her "Mrs. C," she winced again.

Mr. Cater cleared his throat. "Well—er—shall we get on with the little ceremony? I'm sure everyone's anxious to—to—er—this way."

As they all trooped to the far end of the room, one of the brothers pressed a glass of champagne into Gail's hand. "Not like them to forget to offer you a drink," he mumbled, breathing alcohol fumes over her. "I'll say this for them, they serve good booze at their dos."

"You sound as if that's all there is to be said for them."

"Well, load of snobs, aren't they? Thought they were too grand for our Jeannie. That boot-faced mother actually gave us a list of abortion clinics and said they'd 'be responsible for necessary expenses.' I mean, she actually *talks* like that."

"I know," Gail said.

"Well, we weren't having that. We may not be posh, but what's right is right. I said to her straight, when our Dad got Mom in the family way, he did the decent thing and tied the knot, and here we all are, so to speak. So I told her, your David's going to do the decent thing, too, or the four of us is going to know the reason why. Well, it would have been five of us really, 'cause Dad's still a bonny fighting man after the third whiskey.''

"I'm sure he is," Gail murmured. Her eyes were glazing over at these revelations.

"Actually, I think I'd better go and look after Dad. He's getting a bit out of control, if you know what I mean."

Gail knew exactly what he meant. She was feeling stunned by what she'd learned tonight. She looked up and caught Mrs. Cater's eyes upon her. Obviously the older woman guessed what Gail had just heard. The wheel had come full circle. She had rejected Gail as not good enough for her son, and instead had seen him forced to marry into a family of tipsy vulgarians. The bitterness in her eyes was terrible to see. If Gail had wanted revenge she had it at that moment. Instead, it suddenly all seemed so pointless. When she thought of being married to the spineless, foolish David, Gail knew Mrs. Cater had done her a service, however little she had meant to.

She moved along and found herself directly in front of David. "Hallo, David," she said calmly.

"Hallo, Gail."

She sought frantically for something to say. "Are you well?"

"Very well, thank you. And you?"

"I'm fine, thank you."

Then there was a long silence while they stared at each other, with absolutely nothing between them. Neither of them noticed Alex watching them closely.

"Er—well—better be getting along," David said awkwardly.

"Yes," she said. "I wish you the best of luck."

"Can I have your attention, everybody?" Mr. Cater called out. "As you all know, Cater and Son was started by my late father. For a long time I was 'Son,' then I took over when he retired. I've always looked forward to the day when I'd take my own son into full partnership, and now that that day has arrived, we invited our friends along to share the moment with us.

"For some time now, David has been running the firm more or less alone, and overseeing our expansion. We've taken over other businesses, consolidated, and under David's excellent—I might almost say inspired—leadership we've reached the point where we dominate the market. All we needed to make that domination complete was our own haulage firm, and that's something that David's shrewd negotiating skills have brought us. Tonight we sign the papers that make Dickson's Haulage part of Cater and Son, and then I shall have great pleasure in completing the formalities that will make David my partner. Please join me in a toast to my son."

Everyone raised their glass in salute to David. His four brothers-in-law, apparently under the impression that they were at a football match, yelled, "Oggi, oggi, oggi. Oi! Oi! Oi!" Mrs. Cater's smile was fixed on with steel rivets. Gail was watching Alex, who regarded the proceedings with a strange little smile. As the toast finished he attracted Mr. Cater's attention. "If I might say a few words..." he suggested.

"Mr. Medway will say a few words first," Mr. Cater called. "He's here to complete the sale of Dickson's Haulage."

Alex went to stand beside David, facing the assembled company. "That's right," he said. "I'm here about the sale of Dickson's Haulage—but not to Cater and

Son. Dickson's was sold to Medway Industries this afternoon."

Mr. Cater frowned. "I don't know what kind of a joke this is supposed to be, but it's very out of place."

"It's no joke," Alex assured him. "Son David's inspired leadership fell a bit short at the last fence." He held up some papers. "These prove my ownership. They were signed this afternoon, in the presence of lawyers." He gave David a jeering grin. "All those shrewd negotiating skills, and nothing to show for it."

Mr. Cater had skimmed through the papers enough to understand them, and was beginning to splutter. "This is the most outrageous—"

"It's business," Alex said flatly. "Dickson wanted cash, not shares, and he was desperate. If you'd given him cash you could have knocked twenty thousand off the price. You didn't read his eyes right."

"You blithering idiot!" Mr. Cater screamed at his son. "You told me you had him over a barrel."

A murmur ran through the crowd. David was opening and closing his mouth like a goldfish. It seemed as though he actually didn't understand what was happening. Gail watched him, appalled, while a dreadful suspicion crept over her.

"What the devil did you mean, coming here like this?" Mr. Cater demanded of Alex.

"It seemed only fair to tell you in person," Alex said innocently.

"You—you—" Mr. Cater was going purple.

He was interrupted by a guffaw from one of Jeannette's brothers, closely followed by the three others. Grins began to run around the crowd. Some made decent efforts to suppress their laughter, but only succeeded in making choking noises instead. Mrs. Cater screamed and burst into tears. Jeannette was looking blankly from her brothers to her husband. "What's going on?" she demanded.

"Nothing," David muttered.

"How can it be nothing when all these people are laughing at you? Does this mean I won't get that fur coat?"

"Shut up," he snarled. David pulled himself together and took a step toward Alex. "I think what you've done is—is—"

"Done," Alex concluded for him. "That's what it is. It's done. Finished. Completed." He turned to Gail. "Shall we go now?"

"Yes," she said furiously. "Yes, I think it's time we went."

She turned and walked away before he could put a hand on her arm. The crowd parted before the fierce glitter in her eyes. But Alex didn't see it. He remained in blissful ignorance of what was about to descend on him until they were outside. Only when they were out of earshot of the house did Gail explode. "I think that was the most disgraceful, despicable, callous..." Words failed her.

"What?" Alex sounded as if he couldn't believe his ears.

"You set him up. You did it like that on purpose."

"And what if I did? Didn't they do something like that to you, once upon a time?" Alex's voice was sharp with disappointment. He wasn't sure what he'd expected. Gratitude? Perhaps not. But appreciation, certainly. He'd slain her dragons for her, and the awkward woman refused to recognize that.

"What they did to me is my business." She seethed. "Did I ask you to get revenge for me? What on earth was the idea, Alex? You must have known ages ago that you were going to buy this haulage firm—''

"Only this afternoon, actually," he said unwisely.

"What does that mean?"

"Nothing," he mumbled hastily, realizing that he was wandering into a quagmire.

"Of course it means something. Why only this afternoon?"

"When you told me about David Cater—the name rang a bell. It was only today that I remembered we'd been after the same firm."

"You did this because of what I told you about him? *Why?*"

How was he to answer her? To come out with the truth and say that he'd been miserably jealous at the thought of her one great love, and the fact that she'd stayed single for his sake—that would have been impossible for his proud nature. It was even hard to admit it to himself. How could he explain the rage that had gripped him at the thought of a man who'd won the treasure of her love, and been stupid enough to throw it away? Nor could he have found words for his driving need to see them together, to watch the look in her eyes when she saw David again.

"Why?" she repeated.

"Does it matter? If you had any gratitude you'd be glad to see the whole family get what was coming to them."

"That's what it was all about," she said, surveying him strangely. "Spitting in the eye of the Cater family."

"For your sake."

"Don't fool yourself, Alex, and don't try to fool me. You don't do anything for anybody's sake except your own. I don't know what this was about—"

Then you should, you maddening woman, he thought furiously. You should be able to guess that I wanted to know if you still love him. And it tears me apart to hear you taking his side against me. You should know all this without being told.

"But it certainly wasn't about making me feel good," Gail concluded. "I know your pride comes into it somewhere, because your pride comes into everything."

"Forget about my pride," he snapped, raw-nerved.

"*You* forget it—if you know how. Pride's at the back of everything, isn't it? That's why you dressed me up in a king's ransom in gold. It wasn't enough to make David look like a fool on his big day. You had to parade me, weighed down with baubles, just to rub it in. Oh, I could..." She turned her head aside so that he couldn't see the sudden tears that had started in her eyes. The disillusion was cruel. She'd actually dared to hope that his heart, as well as his senses, was turning to her, that he was learning trust and perhaps love. And, instead, she'd merely been a pawn in a cruel game. The beautiful gold jewelry seemed to burn her.

"Here," she said in a passionate rage. "Take it."

"What are you doing?"

"Giving it back to you," she said, tearing it off. "It's served its purpose. You can take it back and get a full refund. It was probably hired, anyway."

In the evening light she saw him turn pale. "What a lousy thing to say," he snapped.

She knew it and was ashamed of herself, but he had the gift of bringing out the worst in her. The devil that was driving her now gave another little prod. "On the contrary, I'm complimenting you on your business instincts," she retorted. "You achieved everything you wanted tonight—*on the cheap.*" The sight of the jewels hurt her, not for their value but for what she'd thought they signified. Pain made her cruel. "Take them or I'll toss them in a ditch," she said.

He seized her hand. "I hate waste, or I'd tell you to do your damndest," he shouted. "So now I know where I stand, don't I? It's been interesting finding out."

"I don't know what you're talking about."

"Think about it."

Instead, she reached into her purse and took out her mobile phone. "Now what are you doing?" he demanded.

"Calling a taxi," she replied glacially. "Since we plainly have nothing further to say to each other."

"I am perfectly prepared to take you home."

"I would sooner drive home in a milk float. Do I make myself plain?"

"Perfectly."

"Then good night."

"Good night."

Chapter Ten

On the evening before Sylvia's wedding, Gail made the trip to Gracely Manor to check the reception arrangements with the caterer. She would have preferred not to go, because of the danger of running into Alex, but she wasn't taking any chances with Sylvia's big day. She arrived to find the marquee standing on the green lawn, and overalled men beginning to carry in trestle tables. The setting sun was bathing the old house in a mellow glow, and gentle breezes played with the trees.

"It's going to be a lovely day tomorrow," the marquee owner said. "Perfect weather for a wedding."

Gail nodded. She could see that he was right. After all the troubles that had dogged their engagement, Sylvia and Freddie were finally going to have an ideal wedding. And that was all that mattered, Gail told herself. The fact that she herself was full of sadness and disillusionment was neither here nor there.

She supposed she ought to be grateful to Alex for exorcising her ghosts. But the fact was that the Caters no longer mattered. The incident at their house had drawn a line beneath the whole affair, but even without that, David had faded to nothing, replaced in her heart by Alex himself. Now Alex had shown that her first opinion of him had been correct. He was hard, arrogant and manipulative. He'd even manipulated *her*, convincing her that he'd thawed, while actually using her as a pawn. The hurt and disillusionment dwarfed anything she'd felt for David Cater.

"So there you are."

She looked up quickly, to find Alex standing there, frowning. "I thought you'd have come into the house to see me," he said.

"I'm here to work. Tomorrow is a very big day, and I want everything to go perfectly."

"Is there any reason to suppose that it won't? Does Sylvia have any complaints about me now?"

"No," Gail said crisply. "According to her, you're sweetness and light personified. I told her not to be fooled. I know you better."

"Very funny."

"I'm not being funny. When you're sweetness and light you're at your most dangerous."

"Are we talking about that business with the Caters again?"

"*You're* talking about it. I'm busy."

She turned away, but he stopped her with a firm hand on her arm. "Hasn't this gone far enough?"

"I'd say you went *too* far," she retorted, twisting his words.

"Yes, you made your feelings pretty plain about that. Now can we forget it?"

"You didn't understand a word I said the other night, did you?" she demanded. "To you it was just a storm in a teacup, and now you think it's over and I should just forget it."

"I don't see why it can't be over. If I offended you, I'm sorry, but I can't change what happened now."

"No, and you can't change the kind of person you are, either. That's why I'm upset, because of what it showed me about *you*. And that's why it'll never be over. Nothing really changes, does it?" she added with a rush of bitterness.

"Well, one thing has changed," he said curtly. "I'm ready to get married now."

"Congratulations."

"I mean it. Look—you win."

"I what?" she asked with a dangerous calm that ought to have warned him.

"You win. We'll have the same deal we discussed before—only this time with marriage. Well, why are you staring at me like that? I give in."

"You give in," she repeated slowly. "In other words, you think I've been scheming to marry you all the time."

"Well, no, not exactly—I mean, of course not. But after all—you do believe in marriage—it's your business—"

"And you think there are no depths I wouldn't stoop to to sell another wedding? Thanks."

"Now, look—"

"And while we're on the subject, we did not *discuss* a deal. You offered me an insulting arrangement and I slapped your face, which I'm strongly tempted to do now."

"Because I want to marry you?" he demanded in outrage.

"Because you suggest marriage in a way that's almost as big an insult as your original proposition," she said, seething.

"How can an offer of marriage be an insult?" he snapped.

"The mere fact that you refer to it as an offer is enough to show you have an attitude problem. When a man is really eager to marry a woman he doesn't *offer* marriage as if he was tossing a bone to a dog. This isn't the nineteenth century. You're not doing me a favor by deigning to offer for my hand, although you plainly think you are—"

"You reckon it's *you doing me* a favor, I take it?"

"*If* I condescended to marry you I *would* be doing you a favor, because I'd be saving you from a life of lonely bachelordom. But I'm not in the mood to do you favors, nor do I think you're worth saving. So I suggest you take your apartment, your jewels, your gold credit card and all the other goodies that you fancy make you so irresistible, and offer them to some woman who's really desperate. And good luck!"

"Well, I think that says it all."

"I should hope so."

As the marquee owner had predicted, the weather was perfect for Sylvia's wedding day. As soon as Gail put her head out of her bedroom window and felt the early morning sun already warm on her face, she knew it was the start of a heat wave. She showered and put on the peach silk suit she'd chosen for the day.

She had a quick breakfast of fruit and coffee, then drove over to Gracely Manor to help Sylvia. As she ar-

rived she noted with satisfaction that the whole com-
plicated operation was already beginning to stir into life.
The huge catering vans were lumbering slowly across the
lawn to take up position just outside the marquee,
which stood dazzling white in the sunshine. Inside those
vans, carefully refrigerated to exactly the right temper-
ature, were gallons of the finest champagne and food
for three hundred guests. An army of waiters and wait-
resses were carrying snowy tablecloths into the marquee to cover the trestle tables. Three florists' vans were
already there, with assistants busily engaged in ferry-
ing flowers into the marquee, to transform a tent into a
palace.

Gail went straight up to Sylvia's room, and found her
sitting in her slip, waiting to put on her wedding gown.
Gail helped her on with it, and stood back as Sylvia
turned slowly before the long mirror, studying her appearance from every angle. "It's perfect," she announced.

"Yes," Gail agreed. "It's perfect." She could see now
that Sylvia's instinct had been correct. Whereas the
luxury of Barry's creations had overwhelmed her, the
simple dress suited her admirably, expressing something about her sweet nature.

But a shadow crossed Sylvia's face. "You don't mind,
do you, Gail—about it not being the dress you chose?"

"Of course not, darling. What matters is that you
should have the dress *you* want. I'm only sorry I forced
my choice on you." She smiled wanly. "I must be getting as bad as Alex."

"I think the two of you are perfect for each other,"
Sylvia said with a warm smile. "I'm all impatience,
waiting for your wedding."

"Don't hold your breath. There isn't going to be one."

"Of course there is," Sylvia said serenely. "He'll ask you any day now."

Gail placed herself in front of Sylvia, her eyes kindling. "I should have said that *you're* as bad as Alex," she said wrathfully. "You both assume that I'm just hanging on to be asked like some lovesick maiden who'll go into a decline if she isn't wanted. Let me tell you, I have better things to do with my life."

"Nonsense!" Sylvia said calmly.

Gail stared at the realization that her gentle cousin had flatly contradicted her—something unheard of. But Sylvia's confidence had been growing by leaps and bounds recently, she realized. "I beg your pardon?"

"I said nonsense," Sylvia repeated. "If you love a man, there isn't anything better to do with your life than marry him."

"Who says I love him?"

"Nobody needs to say it. And when you said that he and I both assume that you're hanging on to be asked—docs that mean he *has* asked you?"

"I wouldn't describe it as asking. He informed me, in a condescending manner, that I'd won—as if I'd been compcting for him."

"Well, that's just his way, isn't it? He's a bit uncivilized, but you can take care of that after you're married."

Gail gave up. Sylvia was a happy bride, about to join her life forever to the man she loved. In other words, she'd moved onto another planet, one where love conquered all problems.

"Maybe," she said vaguely, closing the argument.

There was a knock on the door and Rex Broadbent came in, exclaiming at the sight of his daughter. Sylvia rushed into his arms. Carol followed close behind her father.

"I daren't let him out of my sight," she murmured, indicating Rex. "When he knew Sylvia was marrying into a rich family he thought Christmas had come."

Gail groaned. "Carol, he hasn't—?"

"He has. A loan he calls it, but I said, 'You won't get it back, because Dad never pays back.' He was decent about it, said not to worry and we were all family now."

"That sounds just like Sir James, but—"

"Not, not Sir James. His son."

"Oh, heavens!"

"But he was nice—said not to tell Sylvia anything about it. *Dad,*" Carol shrieked suddenly. "Put that cigar away!"

"Sir James gave it to me," her father protested, aggrieved.

"Not to smoke near Sylvia's dress..."

Carol bustled away with the confiscated cigar. The small commotion saved Gail from needing to say any more. Poor Freddie, she reflected, having to start giving handouts to his future father-in-law on the very day of the wedding. What Alex would have made of that!

Liliane knocked and entered. She was gorgeously attired in a floating gown of silk chiffon. It was dappled in shades of blue, mauve and white, and topped off by a huge hat swathed in the same silk. Diamonds adorned Liliane's ears and wrists. Gail guessed the ensemble had been chosen to put the bride in the shade.

"The cars are here," Liliane announced. "Are you ready to go?"

"Quite ready," Sylvia said, taking up her bouquet.

Liliane cast a wry glance at the simplicity of Sylvia's dress. "Are you sure there isn't something missing?" she inquired sweetly.

Once Sylvia would have been intimidated. Now she didn't even notice. "Quite sure," she said. Almost as an afterthought she added, "You look really lovely, Liliane."

At that precise moment it became clear to everyone that Liliane was overdressed. There was nothing actually wrong with the flaunting, extravagant gown and hat, although the diamonds would have looked more suitable with an evening dress. But Sylvia's elegant simplicity had set the tone, and any departure from it was subtly wrong.

Liliane, who was shrewd enough in her narrow-minded way, saw all this as clearly as anyone. Her mouth tightened, then, as if realizing that nothing could disturb Sylvia's poise, she flounced out of the room.

Freddie was to leave first, accompanied by Alex, his best man. The plan had been for Gail to travel with them, but at the last moment she invented some detail that needed her attention, promising to follow in her own car.

"No," Alex said firmly, taking her aside and speaking in a low voice. "This is Sylvia's big day. You can't spoil it."

"I have no intention of spoiling it," she said, also in a low voice. "I'll be there."

"But you don't want to travel with Freddie and me— and with me alone on the way back," he said grimly. "I understand your feelings, but don't you think you should put personal prejudice aside for Sylvia's sake?" When she hesitated he added, "I seem to remember when you gave me the same lecture. Our first meeting, wasn't it?''

"Yes."

"Well, what's sauce for the goose—"

"Very well," she said quickly. "There's no need to say any more."

"Don't worry. I shan't 'insult' you again."

Freddie appeared. His usual cheery confidence had deserted him and he was shaking with nerves. "Everything's all right, isn't it?" he demanded of Gail. "You've seen Sylvia, and she's—I mean, everything's all right—that is—it's all right?"

"She still loves you and she'll be at the church," Gail assured him, correctly interpreting this jumble.

"Are you *sure?*"

"I'm sure. Freddie, she's wearing her wedding dress. That means she's going to a wedding, so stop panicking."

"Have you got the ring?" Freddie demanded of Alex.

"Of course I have."

"Let me see it."

"Look, I've got it."

"Let me see it." Freddie demanded, in the first order he'd ever given his older brother.

Alex sighed and produced the wedding ring.

"Put it away safely," Freddie commanded. "And don't lose it." He wandered away unhappily.

"I begin to think you did me a favor by saying no," Alex murmured.

"I did you a *big* favor," Gail declared, ignoring the little pain in her heart. "I'm glad you realize that."

"Gail—"

"The car's ready. We should be going," she said quickly.

On the journey, Freddie's nervous presence absorbed their attention. Once they reached the church Alex guided him kindly into his place and Gail went to take her place on the other side. The organist was trying out snatches of tunes while the congregation settled.

And then it was time.

Far overhead the organ pealed out the first bars of "The Wedding March." Gail drew a slow, wondering breath as she saw Sylvia begin to walk down the aisle on her father's arm. Sylvia was always pretty, but today she had a radiant beauty. It wasn't merely the transforming effect of the white dress and veil. It had more to do with a little smile that played on her lips, and a look of eagerness in her sparkling eyes as they sought her groom. After all the troubles that had beset her, Sylvia had come at last into her kingdom. She and Freddie had been through the fire together, and emerged with their love stronger. All that was left now was for them to claim each other in the sight of the world.

Sylvia came to a halt next to Freddie, and they stood side by side, in front of the parson. He smiled at them, and began to intone, "Dearly beloved, we are gathered here to join together this man and this woman in holy matrimony...."

Gail found that her sight was suddenly blurred. She couldn't think why, except that she was happy for her cousin. This was how love ought to be, not the nervous hostility of two people who mistrusted each other, and whose love was half antagonism.

She thought of the proposal Alex had made her only a few hours before. She could still accept, and in a few weeks she might be the happy bride, gliding down the aisle. But she couldn't make the vision fit. Not with

Alex. Long before then they'd have got on each other's wrong side, and she would have a second useless wedding dress on her hands. She raised her head a fraction and forced herself to concentrate on the wedding.

When it was Freddie's turn to speak, his voice was quiet, as though the sight of his bride had stunned him. "I, Frederick Anthony, take thee Sylvia Elizabeth, to be my wedded wife, to have and to hold, from this day forward..."

It wouldn't work like that for us, Gail argued with herself. *We'd have and hold each other until the first big quarrel. Our marriage would be one long fight for supremacy. No, on second thoughts it would be a short fight for supremacy, over within a year.*

"I, Sylvia Elizabeth, take thee, Frederick Anthony, to be my wedded husband..."

How certain she sounds! She knows exactly what she's doing. I've always treated her like my kid sister, but now she's found her feet and I'm all of a dither.

"...for richer for poorer, in sickness and in health, to love and to cherish, till death us do part..."

Whoever wrote the marriage service covered all the exits. There isn't a single loophole once you've given those promises. That's why I've made the right decision. I know it's the right decision. I do know it—really.

And then it was over, and the organ swelled to a song of triumph as the bride and groom—now husband and wife—turned and walked together back down the aisle and out into the sunlight.

The photographs seemed to go on forever. In several of them Gail found herself standing close to Alex, smiling to cover her sadness, trying to pretend that his nearness wasn't a strain. But she was longing for the day to end.

She managed to coerce some guests into their car for the journey back, and so was saved from having to make it alone with Alex. His grim expression told her that he fully understood.

Because of the hot weather the sides of the marquee had been rolled up, and delightful breezes wafted over the company that assembled for the wedding breakfast. The huge cake seemed to go up to the sky, topped off by a tiny little bride and groom.

There was no doubt that this was the most successful wedding Gail had ever arranged. Two of the guests asked for her card because of weddings that were about to be settled in their own families. The arrangements went off without a hitch, the bride and groom were blissfully happy. Perhaps the groom's brother was a little tense, but only one person noticed that, and she had her own aching heart to concern her.

When it was time for the speeches Alex, as best man, rose and did his duty perfectly, speaking of Sylvia with a warmth that brought tears to Gail's eyes. Of course, she thought, he was always conscientious, and he was making amends for his past behavior in grand style.

As the light began to fade, everyone moved into the house for dancing. The band struck up. Freddie and Sylvia took the floor together, moving with the perfect union of love, their gazes locked, conscious only of each other. That was how it should be, Gail thought.

Alex came and took her hand firmly. "I really have things to do..." she began to say, but before she'd got the words out she found herself on the dance floor, held close in his arms, the very thing she'd wanted to avoid.

"Go on, say it," he told her with grim humor.

"Say what?"

"I had no right to rush you like that, et cetera, et cetera."

"Well, you hadn't."

"Look, you were going to dance with me anyway, so it was simpler to just cut the arguments and get on with it."

"You're wasting your time," she said. "I'm not going to change my mind."

"If you think I'm dancing with you so that I can beg you to marry me, you're mistaken. I beg from no woman. You should know that."

Gail looked up into his face and her heart sank. This was the old Alex, the harsh, impatient man she'd met that first day, and disliked. "Then let's get the performance over with quickly," she said with a sigh.

"It's not a performance. I did have a reason for wanting to talk to you, and this was the most efficient way of doing it."

"And let's be efficient at all costs," she murmured.

"Precisely. I thought you'd be interested to know what I've found out about Lily. All the worst I suspected of her is true, and then some. She's got another man."

"No!" she said instinctively.

"It's true. That's why she keeps making all these trips to London. She's meeting him. And they've even had a little holiday together—on Dad's credit card, of course."

"I can't believe that—even of Lily."

"Believe it. I'm just waiting for the final piece of evidence."

"And what will you do then?"

"Show her up for what she is. The sooner she's exposed and thrown out, the better. Then Dad can get on with his life."

"Poor Sir James," Gail murmured.

"He'll be hurt at first, but it'll be better for him in the long run. Surely you can see that?"

"What I can see is that you can't wait to be proved right, even if his heart gets broken in the process," she said bitterly. "Hey, what do you think you're doing?" Alex had started to walk off the dance floor, keeping a firm hold on her.

"Come with me," he said. "A maid has just come with a message for Lily and she slipped away as quietly as she could manage. This may be the moment—"

"You can't suppose that she's brought him here," Gail protested.

"All I know is she's acting furtively." He closed the door of the morning room behind them and led her down the corridor. From the end, where there was a telephone, they could hear, but not see, Liliane.

"It's better if you don't call me here..." she was saying urgently. "I'll call you when it's safe...yes, darling...we can meet next week...."

"I think not," Alex said, laying his hand over the rest and cutting off the call.

Liliane gave a violent gasp and her wild eyes went from Alex's face to Gail's.

"This has gone on long enough," Alex said coldly. "I've suspected what you're up to for a good while, and now I have no doubt." His face grew dark with anger. "To think you've been deceiving my father all this time—just as I knew you would. All these convenient little trips away—only he doesn't know who you really meet, does he? And he trusts you, so he doesn't ask where the money goes."

"Don't tell him," Liliane begged. "You don't understand—"

"I think I do. The sooner he knows, the better. Then we can get you out of this house and forget you."

"But he won't forget me," Liliane said with a touch of defiance. "Jamie loves me."

"He won't when he knows the truth," Alex said grimly. "Don't try to talk me out of it. I've waited too long for this moment."

Liliane put up her hands as if to implore him. It was no use, Gail thought. It would take more than her pleas to move that granite heart. But before any of them could speak again they heard Sir James's voice from the far end of the corridor. "I don't know where she vanished to," he was saying. "Perhaps she's down here. Liliane, are you there?"

The next moment he reached them. He stopped, letting his gaze run around the little group by the telephone, and his eyes visibly softened as they rested on his wife. "There you are, darling. I wondered what had happened to you."

"I just—remembered something—that I—"

"Why, you're all upset." Sir James moved closer to study her face. "Whatever's the matter? Have you been crying?"

Time seemed to stop as Gail's eyes flew to Alex's face. Liliane too was watching him, waiting for the blow to fall. But it didn't happen. To her astonishment Gail saw that Alex was riven with indecision. The next moment he forced himself to grin and give a laugh that sounded almost natural. "Of course she's been crying,'' he said. "Women always cry at weddings, otherwise they feel they haven't enjoyed themselves.''

Sir James put his hands on Liliane's shoulders and searched her face. "Is that all it is?'' he asked.

"Of course,'' she said in a voice that quivered. "It's been such a lovely wedding, and Sylvia's a beautiful bride—''

"Not as beautiful as you were,'' he said warmly, smiling into her eyes. "Do you remember our day?''

"Oh, yes, Jamie darling.''

He kissed her. "Come on, let's get back to our guests.'' He put his arm around his wife and they went away together. It seemed to Gail that she was leaning on him.

"Why didn't you do it?'' she asked.

"Because I couldn't,'' he said, scowling. "When it came to the point, I couldn't destroy his happiness so brutally.''

"Perhaps you've paid that debt you felt you owed him, after you disappointed him at the circus. You always wanted to make it up to him, and now you have.''

"I suppose I have. It sticks in my craw to shield that woman, but Dad comes first.''

Gail nodded. "Yes,'' she agreed.

"But I won't answer for myself the next time,'' he said grimly.

Sylvia appeared at the end of the corridor, waving to Gail. "Come and help me change,'' she said.

Upstairs she threw her arms about Gail. "It was a beautiful wedding,'' she whispered. "Thank you for everything.''

"And it's going to be a beautiful honeymoon,'' Gail assured her. "Let's get you off.''

As they removed the wedding dress Sylvia said, "What were you and Alex whispering about? Have you made up?"

"No. Nothing's really changed. I can't marry a man who could do what he did the other night."

Sylvia sat down in her slip. "Tell me about it," she said as though their roles were reversed, and she was now the giver of advice.

"Not now. You've got to get dressed. Freddie's waiting."

"I won't move a step until you tell me," Sylvia said calmly.

Gail gave her an account of the night at the Caters' house, and how Alex had made a fool of David. "And he actually had the nerve to try to pretend he'd done it for me," she said. "I never asked him to."

"Of course not. He did it for himself," Sylvia said.

"Only because he has to be one-up on everybody—"

"Nonsense," Sylvia said again. "You're being awfully dense suddenly, Gail. He wanted to see you and David together, of course."

"Why should he?"

"Because he needed to know if you were still in love with David. He's jealous."

"You wouldn't say that if you'd seen him," Gail said darkly. "He was enjoying himself."

"Then you probably showed that you're not in love with David any more. Or are you?"

"Of course not. I had a lucky escape there."

"Maybe Alex felt you should know that. Maybe he needs to know that you know it. You're being awfully stupid about this, darling."

"It's too late," Gail said unhappily. "It's all over between us. Now that you're married we won't have to see each other anymore. We'll soon forget."

There was no time to say more. Hurriedly they got Sylvia into her going-away clothes. Freddie came knocking at the door and they ran down the stairs together. Sylvia's bouquet was still in the hall and she seized it up and tossed it directly at Gail. Then she was gone, running down the steps to the waiting car, hand in hand with her new husband.

Conscious of Alex's cool eyes on her, Gail studied the bouquet without looking up. Mechanically she assessed the state of the flowers, and decided that the florist wasn't up to standard this time. Or perhaps it was just her imagination that the lovely blooms, which had seemed to promise so much, had already started to wilt.

Chapter Eleven

Sylvia and Freddie seemed to have taken summer with them. Almost at once a rainstorm set in, and the skies were gray for several days. The weather reflected Gail's mood, for her heart had grown heavy. She couldn't help loving Alex, but she'd rejected him, sure that their future would hold only sadness and a parting. Passion alone was not enough. There had to be sympathy of the heart, and it seemed that they had very little of that.

Then something happened that threw her into disarray. Sylvia called from the honeymoon chalet in Switzerland, brimming with happiness. When she'd eulogized her new husband for a while she allowed him to take over the phone to thank Gail, yet again, for "the wonderful work you did on the wedding."

"I want to thank you, too," she said.

"Thank me for what?"

"Sylvia can't hear any of this, can she?"

"No, the chambermaid's just come in and she's talking to her. What is it, Gail?"

"I heard that Rex touched you for money on the wedding day. It was nice of you to keep it quiet from Sylvia—"

"Hang on, Rex didn't touch me for money."

"Carol said he did. At least . . ." A horrible thought had suddenly come to Gail. Carol had simply said "the son." But surely . . .

"I saw Rex talking to Alex," Freddie said, "and I think money passed because Alex put his hand into his pocket. Well, well! Rex is an old devil, isn't he?"

"You mean Alex gave him money?" Gail asked frantically.

"Well, it wasn't me, so perhaps it was Alex. It was decent of him not to let Sylvia know. When you think what he'd have made of it at one time . . ."

"Yes," Gail said slowly.

She put the phone down and sat in silence, thinking about this and about the unexpected generosity Alex had shown to Liliane and his father. Deep down, at some level few people were ever allowed to see, Alex understood that people's feelings came first. He didn't often talk about it. But he knew it.

Another memory came back to her. Alex, apologizing to Sylvia in the hospital, begging her to marry Freddie, saying, "When you love someone, there are no 'buts.'" And the performance he'd put on at the Caters' was cruel, but the cruelty of a man driven by jealous love. It was easy to see that now. Gail dropped her head in her hands and it swept over her like a wave of misery that she'd made a terrible mistake. Love had held out its hands to her, and she'd turned away because she hadn't known. When you loved someone there were no "buts."

There *ought* to be no buts. And Alex had understood that better than herself.

The phone rang on her desk. She answered it automatically.

"Mrs. Blake is on the line," Jan said.

"Tell her I'll talk to her in a minute," Gail replied in a husky voice.

"Are you all right?"

"Yes, I'm fine. It's just—I need a moment."

When she'd recovered, she forced herself to talk brightly to the customer. Then she took her car keys and went into the outer office, thinking up reasons for needing to go out. She had to get away to think.

But as she glanced at the window that looked out onto the street she saw Liliane's face staring back at her from the other side of the glass. Before the tide of dislike had time to rise she noted how wretched and ill Liliane appeared. The other woman saw her and raised a tentative hand, almost in appeal, it seemed to Gail. The next moment Liliane's eyes had closed and she'd fallen to the pavement.

Gail signaled to Jan and they hurried outside. They took Liliane into a cool room at the rear, equipped with a comfortable couch and a small bathroom directly next door. Her eyes were still closed, her face a greenish color and she leaned on them heavily to walk. She was shaking as she dropped to the couch.

"Fetch some strong, sweet tea and then leave us alone," Gail said to Jan.

After a moment Liliane came round. Her elegant clothes were untidy and her makeup was smudged, but she seemed past caring. "Lie still," Gail said. "Don't try to say anything, yet."

A sudden wild look came into Liliane's eyes. Gail reacted fast, guiding her to the bathroom just in time, and leaving her in privacy until the storm had passed. When Liliane emerged she looked shattered, but was a slightly better color. "The tea's arrived," Gail said. "Have some before you say anything."

Liliane sat passively, like a forlorn little girl, while Gail settled the cup and saucer in her hand and encouraged her to drink. She looked completely different from the worldly-wise young woman she'd always seemed before, and Gail found herself almost liking her.

"Does Jimmy know?" Gail asked.

Liliane shook her head.

"Is there a problem about that?" Gail said delicately.

"It's his baby, if that's what you mean," Liliane said with a faint touch of defiance. "But I know none of you will believe me."

"We'll believe you if it's true."

"Alex won't. He won't want to believe me. He won't want me to have a Medway baby. He thinks my family isn't good enough for the Medways."

"It's not that. It's the man who—I mean the one who—"

"What man?"

"The one we heard you talking to on the phone—saying he wasn't to call you at home—"

Liliane was staring at her. "But that wasn't—you mean Alex thought—?"

"If it wasn't a man, who was it?"

Liliane's eyes filled with tears. "It was my Mom."

"What? But I thought your parents were dead?"

Liliane shook her head. "Dad left when I was eight. Mom and I never saw him again. She brung—*brought* me up on her own—always wanted the best for me. When I got married she told me to say she was dead. She said she didn't want to get in my way. I see her whenever I can, and I send her money. We even managed a weekend away together. It's just—just..." Liliane's mouth wobbled, "Now I'm going to have a baby, and there's nobody to talk to—nobody likes me—"

"That's not true," Gail said helplessly. Apart from Sir James, it *was* true, but she could hardly say so.

"It is." Liliane wept. "I tried so hard to be a proper 'ladyship,' but I've just made a mess of it."

"You didn't have to try to be anything. All Jimmy wanted was you, as you were."

"Lily Hatch who grew up in the gutter," Liliane said in a choked voice.

"But *he* started by selling fruit off a barrow. He loves you, *you*."

"I know but—but—" a quiver went over Liliane's face and a loud wail broke from her "—*I want my Mom*."

The cup of tea spilled all over the floor as she flung herself face down into the sofa and sobbed her heart out. Gail looked at her sympathetically for a moment, then went outside to find Jan.

"Get me Sir James on the phone," she said.

At first she refused Sir James's invitation to dinner, but he pleaded. "A man's first meeting with his mother-in-law, Gail. I need some moral support."

"You'll have the rest of the family."

"Sylvia and Freddie are still on honeymoon and Alex is abroad at the moment. *Please*, Gail."

"All right, I'll be there."

Liliane's mother turned out to be a dumpy little woman, blissfully proud of her daughter. Liliane too seemed to have discarded some restraint and showed more pleasure in her husband's society than Gail could ever recall seeing. It was all too clear now that she loved him as the replacement of the father who'd deserted her. But at least that was genuine love, which nobody had ever credited her with before. And when he said he hoped their child would be a girl Liliane's happiness was complete.

The crowning touch to the evening was a call from Sylvia and Freddie, about to start the journey home. Amid the rejoicing and toasts Gail quietly took her leave and departed. She had no part in this happy family scene. She'd never felt so lonely in her life.

Alex saw the change in Sylvia on his next visit home. It wasn't just that her honeymoon had left her lightly tanned. She'd also gained in maturity and assurance, no longer seeming overwhelmed by the big house, or by Liliane or by himself. It now seemed natural to seek her out and ask her advice.

"What do you think of Lily now?" he demanded.

"I think we were all a little hard on her," Sylvia said. "She lost her way, but she's found it again. Everything will be all right."

"Hard on her? After she set the dogs on you?"

"Weren't they the same dogs you set on her?" Sylvia reminded him. "And they weren't even very efficient dogs, since they didn't manage to find out that her mother was still alive. *She's* forgiven *you*."

"Good of her," he said dryly.

"And look how happy your father is."

"Yes," Alex said slowly. "Yes, I know."

"It'll take just two more things to complete his happiness. One is to have a daughter."

"Having already two great lummocks for sons," Alex observed with a faint grin.

"As you say. And the other thing is you and Gail. He's longing to see you two married, you know."

"He should save his energy. That's one marriage he'll never see. You probably don't know this, but..." Alex stopped, choking over the admission of a rejection. "Well, never mind," he said at last.

"She turned you down." Sylvia supplied the answer for him. "I knew. She told me."

"Did she tell you why? She didn't tell *me*—not in any terms that I could understand, anyway."

"She told you all right. If you didn't understand—well, perhaps you *can't* understand, and she was right to turn you down. You do seem to go about everything like a bull in a china shop."

"Thanks."

"Gail has suffered enough from people who act like that. You obviously know about David Cater—"

"Does she think I'm the same kind of weakling?" Alex demanded, outraged.

"No, a different kind," Sylvia said calmly.

He scowled. "No one's ever called me a weakling before."

"I think it's pretty weak to be so eaten up with pride that you bulldoze your way through everything and everyone because you're afraid of what will happen if you don't. After what happened last time Gail went to church to marry, she needs someone who's going to coax her into taking the risk of trying it again, not a caveman who's going to drag her there by the hair."

"That's a lot of amateur psychology you're spouting, Sylvia—"

"You were even too weak a moment ago to admit that Gail had turned you down. From all accounts you didn't even ask her properly, just tried to hand down an edict from on high. You're afraid to risk being rejected and vulnerable, and that's the biggest weakness of all." Sylvia stopped herself and stared at Alex. "To think I actually used to be scared of you. I can't imagine it now."

"Neither can I," he said grimly.

"Then I'll go a step further, Alex, and tell you that you have no humility."

"What the devil has humility got to do with it?"

"What I'm saying is that until Gail means more to you than your pride, you'll never win her."

He set his jaw. "Then I'll do without her."

Chapter Twelve

The weather settled into the most beautiful autumn Gail could remember. The green of the trees was being replaced by crimson, orange, yellow and brown. Gail stood watching as 'her' brides were photographed beneath these glorious canopies, and later studied the pictures, trying to note impersonally how the white dresses glowed against the richly colored backgrounds. But her heart kept seeing the brides' smiles, and the happy, radiant looks on their faces.

It might have been her. She might have been the young woman standing beneath the trees, laughing as her veil flew up in the breeze; or the other one, hand in hand with her groom, gazing at him with eyes full of adoration.

No, she stopped there. Those happy brides could never have been her. They had married men who loved them more than themselves, men who counted nothing of importance if they could only have the woman they loved. The man that Gail's heart was stubbornly set on, resisting all attempts to dislodge him, wanted her only on his own terms. She could never have stood beside him, glowing radiantly into the future, confident that she was loved by a man who prized her above all the world. And without that, marriage would only be a cruel deception.

But then she would remember that there was another side to Alex, one that had showed itself several times, and that her love could have brought out completely. Ah, well! It was too late for regrets now.

The final touch, if any were needed, came when Sylvia, fresh back from her honeymoon, came to see her and told her about her conversation with Alex. "I told him that until you meant more to him than his pride, he'd never win you," she said. "And he just glared in that stony way he has—"

"I know it," Gail said, her heart sinking.

"And said, 'Then I'll do without her.'"

Gail smiled wanly. "So you see, I did the right thing in turning him down."

"Yes, I'm afraid you did."

Gail, too, thought Sylvia had altered. At one time the painful little story she'd just recounted would have been kept to herself out of care for Gail's feelings. But now the happiness of the new wife seemed to encase her in armor, deadening her ability to feel empathy. Gail wouldn't have expected it of her. Nor would she have expected Sylvia's next bright remark. "The best thing you can do is to forget about him completely. You'll soon find someone else."

"I don't think I ever want anyone else," Gail said with a touch of bitterness.

"Oh, you'll soon snap out of that. Freddie and I are going to visit some friends of his this weekend, and we want you to come with us."

"How can I be away over a weekend?"

"We'll collect you on Saturday evening when the wedding you're working on is over."

"I usually like to go to church on Sunday morning," Gail mused.

"Goodness, don't you get enough of churches, working in them all the time?" Sylvia said with a laugh. "Now, no arguments. You need a break."

Gail was too bewildered by her cousin's insensitivity to argue much further, and before she knew it she'd agreed. She regretted it as soon as the words were out of her mouth, but it was too late, for Sylvia swept away in a whirl of arrangements. The following weekend Gail spent the Sunday with Sylvia and Freddie at a house in the country where everyone was very bright and cheerful, and everything jarred on Gail's nerves. She thought how nice it would have been to go to St. Anthony's, the little country church where she usually attended morning service, and promised herself that she wouldn't miss it again.

But she did miss it the following week, because Jan unaccountably mislaid some urgent papers and they had to spend the whole of Sunday searching for them.

She was in the middle of the autumn rush, when people hurried to marry before winter closed in. Sylvia returned to lend a hand. "Freddie got indignant and said I didn't need to work but I told him not to be so old-fashioned," she said. "Anyway, it's just until the baby's born." She patted her stomach.

"Already?" Gail asked in wonder.

"It's too soon for a doctor to be sure, but *I* know," Sylvia said triumphantly. "Liliane and I spend half our time with our heads together these days. She's ever so much nicer now she's found her feet. She's really beginning to bulge now. You'll be amazed when you see her on Sunday."

"On Sunday?"

"At lunch. Her mother's coming to meet Freddie and me because we were still on honeymoon for her first visit. Oh, don't say I didn't tell you."

"Not a word."

"Thank goodness it came out in time. We're having a big lunch party on Sunday. Don't worry, Alex won't be there. He's in Australia."

"But I can't—"

"Oh, darling, please don't refuse to come. I'll be in such trouble for forgetting to tell you. It's all settled. Be there at eleven in the morning. Bye now."

Gail had half feared that this was a trick to bring her and Alex together, and she would turn up to find him present. But there was no sign of him. Which was a relief, of course, but there was a little ache in her heart just the same. It would have been nice to see him again and draw a line under the past. She would have liked to know how he'd reacted to the news about Liliane and how he got on with her now. With a little effort it might have been possible to meet as friends. But it seemed he wanted nothing more to do with her.

It was one of those days when everything seemed determined to go wrong. Sylvia called in to say that she was feeling poorly and wouldn't be in to work. Jan telephoned to say she'd be a bit late, and "a bit" stretched into a whole morning. Luckily two of her assistants had a lot of office work to do that day, and their presence was a help, but Gail was still beginning to feel frazzled when the phone rang again.

"Gail, it's Jan."

"Where on earth are you?"

"I bumped into Mrs. Hammond. You're doing her daughter's wedding."

"Yes, I remember. It's at St. Anthony's—"

"We're all there now. She doesn't think it's going to be big enough—"

"But I've already told her there's room for everyone—"

"Yes, but now she's seen the building again, she doesn't believe you. She's getting hysterical. She won't calm down unless you get out here yourself."

"That woman's impossible—"

"I know, but just humor her."

"All right, I'll be right there."

She hurried out into her car and drove the short distance to St. Anthony's. It was set in the country, an old-fashioned little church built six hundred years ago of gray stone. Rooks cawed in its tall elms, and several generations of parishioners slept peacefully beneath stones that had grown crooked with the years. The way in was through an old oak gateway. Beyond it the path was covered in red and brown leaves. More leaves floated down onto the car as Gail drove through.

There was so sign of anyone, but the church door was open. A rustling sound caught her attention and she turned just in time to see a black and white figure scuttling between the trees. Then it was gone. Gail rubbed her eyes. For a moment she'd almost thought she'd seen the vicar, dressed in full regalia, sidling past as if trying to escape detection. But that made no sense.

"Hello," she called, making her way into the church. Light streamed in colored rays through the stained glass windows, down onto the black-and-white flagstones and the ancient tombs with their carved figures of knights and ladies. There was no sign of anyone, and yet Gail had the strangest feeling of the air being alive. "Is anybody there?" she called.

"Yes," Alex said.

She turned quickly and found him standing behind her. There was no time to still the mad beating of her heart, or to stop the color flooding into her face. She knew he must see how affected she was. It took a while for her to be able to talk without sounding breathless.

"I wasn't expecting to find you here. I was called out on a job—"

"I know," he said.

Suddenly Jan stepped out of the shadows. "I'm afraid I slandered poor Mrs. Hammond," she confessed. "She isn't here."

Before Gail could say anything Sylvia appeared through an oak door. "This is all about a different wedding," she said. "We have a rather unusual situation, and as you're the expert it seemed best to consult you."

More doors, the sound of rustling movements growing closer. Suddenly everyone seemed to be there—not only Jan and Sylvia, but also Freddie, Sir James and a smiling Liliane, and Liliane's mother. Barry was there, too, grinning from ear to ear.

"What—what is the unusual situation?" Gail asked breathlessly.

Alex took her shoulders and turned her. "You'll find a clue written on that wall behind you," he said.

Gail whirled to where Sylvia was pointing to a church notice board, where there was a list of the marriage banns that were being read out in the Sunday services. Dazed, Gail took in the words: between Alexander James Medway, bachelor, and Gail Frances Rivers, spinster. If any of you know just cause or impediment why these two persons should not be joined together in holy matrimony, ye are to declare it. This is the third time of asking.

"The *third* time of asking," she murmured.

"It wasn't easy keeping you away three Sundays in a row," Alex explained.

Gail's eyes sought Sylvia. "You knew about this?" she accused.

"Of course," Sylvia confessed, her eyes dancing with glee. "It's been so hard keeping the secret, but we managed it."

"And who thought up this brilliant idea?"

"He did!"

"She did!"

Alex and Sylvia spoke together, each indicating the other. Then they laughed like conspirators. Gail ran her hand distractedly through her hair. "You told me," she said to Sylvia, "that Alex said he could do without me. In fact you went out of your way to tell me that."

"Right," she agreed. "But what I didn't tell you was that the next moment he took it all back and asked me to find a way through to you. I promised to help."

"She said we had to take you by surprise, so that you didn't have time to argue—on account of your being so bossy and overbearing," Alex explained, with something in his eyes that might almost have been a twinkle. "So here we are," he prompted. "Everything's here except the bride. You're the wedding expert. What do you suggest?"

Before Gail could collect her thoughts the vicar bustled in, fully attired. "Are we all ready?" he asked, beaming.

"Not quite," Gail told him.

"I was told the wedding would be at two o'clock, and it's nearly that now."

"But you all forgot something," Gail said. "Read what it says up there about 'just cause and impediment.'" Gail raised her voice and announced to the whole church, "I declare the existence of an impediment."

"Oh dear!" The vicar's brow furrowed.

"There's no impediment," Freddie declared at once. "I've got the ring—"

"And I've got the license," Alex said, producing it.

"And I'm going to give the bride away," Sir James said.

"There *is* an impediment," Gail insisted. "The impediment is called Alex Medway."

"I thought he was the groom," the vicar said, trying to keep up.

"He is also the impediment," Gail declared. "Because he's so high-handed and arrogant that he dared to announce my marriage without even asking me—"

"I did ask you," Alex reminded her. "You said no. It was plainly a waste of time talking to you, so I just went ahead."

His effrontery took her breath away. "And you have the nerve to demand that I marry you—?"

"Not demand," he said quickly. "Beg."

Before all of them he went down on one knee, taking her hand and looking up at her. "Please marry me,

Gail," he said, "because I can't live without you. And I told you a lie. I didn't do this because you're bossy—although you are—I did it because of what happened to you that other time. This way it's *my* pride on the line, not yours. If this wedding doesn't happen *I'm* the one who'll look like a clown. But I hope it does happen—because I love you very much, and I want you for my wife."

Suddenly Gail was struck dumb. She, who'd never been at a loss for words, found her heart so full that her brain wouldn't function. There was only room for feelings of overflowing, passionate love for this man who'd sacrificed his pride—his most precious possession—to exorcise her ghost. His love shone from his eyes, reaching out to encompass and envelope her, making her heart sing with joy. When you really loved someone, there were no "buts."

The only thing she could find to say, in a shaking voice, was, "Do get up from those flagstones. You'll get dust on your knees."

He rose and looked around at the assembled company, watching the scene in various attitudes of tense expectation. Sylvia and Freddie were holding their breath, Liliane was clutching her husband's arm as if the suspense was too much to bear. Suddenly a transforming grin broke across Alex's face.

"It's all right, everyone," he told them. "She's said yes."

A cheer broke from the little crowd as he swept her fiercely into his embrace for an overwhelming kiss. Her last doubts were gone. Gail threw her arms ecstatically about him and put her heart into that kiss. There were so many things they had to say to each other, but those could wait. For now the only messages that counted were the ones passing between their lips and their hearts. She saw the relief in his eyes. He'd been desperately afraid that his gamble would fail, and that fear told her the depth of his love more surely than words could ever do.

The vicar coughed discreetly. The sound galvanized the little company into life. Sylvia claimed Gail and shepherded her firmly into a little room where Barry was unpacking the glittering wedding dress that Gail had worn for her "first" wedding to Alex. Liliane bustled in and started removing Gail's street clothes, clucking like a mother hen. Maternity, and the sense of security she gained from her husband, had transformed her. Shyly she handed Gail a blue silk rosette.

"Something borrowed, something blue," she said. "You can pin it onto your slip."

"Pin it on for me," Gail said, smiling.

At last the dressing was complete and they all stood back to admire. "I knew it," Barry said with a happy sigh. "That dress was always wrong for Sylvia, but perfect for you."

Regarding herself in the mirror Gail realized that Sylvia had been right all along. Subconsciously she'd chosen a wedding dress for herself, which meant that she'd intended to marry Alex for some time, perhaps from the very beginning.

There was a knock and Sir James called, "Are you ready? Can I come in?"

His eyes glowed at the sight of Gail, and he tucked her hand through his arm. "You just wait until you see the reception at the manor," he said.

"But I haven't—" she began involuntarily.

"But I have," Sylvia said. "You taught me well. Here's your bouquet." She hurried away to her seat, followed by Barry.

Overhead the organ pealed out the first bars of "The Wedding March." Sir James patted her hand as they moved out into the church, and turned down the aisle. There was the altar, and there in front of it was Alex, his face turned toward her, looking anxious.

Slowly Gail moved forward, her eyes fixed on him. It was there, as she had known it would be—the look she'd seen on his face in the mock wedding—a look of utter and total devotion. The years stretched before them, years in which he might speak of love only rarely, if at all, but in which his proud heart would always be hers.

As she neared him he smiled and held out his hand to her. Now they were close she saw more than love in his eyes. She saw also triumph that he had finally secured her for himself.

Side by side, they stood before the vicar, and he raised his voice.

"Dearly beloved, we are gathered here to join together this man and this woman...."

*   *   *   *   *

COMING NEXT MONTH

#1084 MAKE ROOM FOR BABY—Kristin Morgan
Bundles of Joy
Once, Camille Boudreaux and Bram Delcambre dreamed of marriage—until betrayal tore them apart. But with a new baby about to join them together as a family, would their love get a second chance?

#1085 DADDY LESSONS—Stella Bagwell
Fabulous Fathers
Joe McCann was about to fire Savanna Starr until he saw her skill at child rearing. Would helping this single dad raise his teenage daughter lead to a new job—as his wife?

#1086 WILDCAT WEDDING—Patricia Thayer
Wranglers and Lace
Nothing would get between Jessie Burke and her ranch. Not even dynamic oilman Brett Murdock. But Brett had more on his mind than Jessie's land. He wanted Jessie—for life.

#1087 HIS ACCIDENTAL ANGEL—Sandra Paul
Spellbound
Bree Smith was supposed to teach cynical Devlin Hunt about love—not fall for the handsome bachelor! What chance did an angel like her have with a man who didn't believe in miracles?

#1088 BELATED BRIDE—Charlotte Moore
Karen Haig had left her hometown a jilted bride years ago. Now she was back—and her former fiancé Seth Bjornson had a plan to make her stay. But could she trust her heart to Seth again?

#1089 A CONVENIENT ARRANGEMENT—Judith Janeway
Debut Author
Jo Barnett might be sharing a home with Alex MacHail but she wasn't about to share her life with him. Then Alex introduced her to his adorable little boy, and Jo found herself falling for father and son.

Take 4 bestselling love stories FREE

Plus get a FREE surprise gift!

HE'S MORE THAN A MAN, HE'S ONE OF OUR

DADDY LESSONS
Stella Bagwell

Joe McCann didn't need anybody telling him how to be a good father. Especially not his outspoken secretary, Savanna Star. Why, he was just about to fire her! But he had to admit he did need help on the home front. And Savanna *had* managed to capture his daughter's heart. But no woman—especially not Savanna—was going to steal his heart, too.

Look for *Daddy Lessons* in June, from Silhouette Romance.

Fall in love with our **Fabulous Fathers!**

Silhouette
R O M A N C E™

Continuing in May from

Silhouette ROMANCE™

by
Carolyn Zane

When twin sisters trade places, mischief, mayhem
and romance are sure to follow!

You met Erica in UNWILLING WIFE (SR#1063).
Now Emily gets a chance to find her perfect man in:

WEEKEND WIFE (SR#1082)

Tyler Newroth needs a wife—just for the weekend. And
kindhearted Emily Brant can't tell him no. But she soon
finds herself wishing this temporary marriage was for real!

Don't miss this wonderful continuation of the
SISTER SWITCH series. Available in May—only from

Silhouette ROMANCE™

SSD2

Announcing
the New Pages & Privileges™ Program
from Harlequin® and Silhouette®

Get All This FREE
With Just One Proof-of-Purchase!

- **FREE Travel Service** with the guaranteed lowest available airfares plus 5% cash back on every ticket

- **FREE Hotel Discounts** of up to 60% off at leading hotels in the U.S., Canada and Europe

- **FREE Petite Parfumerie** collection (a $50 Retail value)

- **FREE $25 Travel Voucher** to use on any ticket on any airline booked through our Travel Service

- **FREE Insider Tips Letter** full of fascinating information and hot sneak previews of upcoming books

- **FREE Mystery Gift** (if you enroll before May 31/95)

And there are more great gifts and benefits to come!
Enroll today and become Privileged!

(see insert for details)

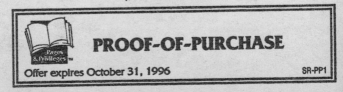